Scars

Eileen Dorcey

Cover artwork by Kelly O'Toole

Doris,

So thankful to

Rockin' Horse Ranch

another (leisurely) road

trip someday?

Love,

Eileen M Dorcey

DEDICATION

This book belongs to Jerry Quinn without whose technical knowledge, infinite patience, and unwavering support it would still be sitting on my computer.

ACKNOWLEDGMENTS

I would like to thank my readers for spotting the errors, making intelligent suggestions, and believing in this project.

Special thanks to Bill Jajic, who, in the eleventh hour, took on the project of reading and editing this book. For someone he's never met. A real-life hero in my mind.

To Jan Malin, art teacher, for giving the cover design of this book as a project to her students.

Kelly O'Toole for creating the artwork that graces the cover.

While based on real life experiences, this book is purely
fiction. Any resemblance to persons living or dead is
coincidental.

"After all it's what we've done,
That makes us what we are."

Jim Croce, 1972, One Less Set of Footsteps on Your Floor in the Morning

1

MORNING RIDE

 It's dark and she can barely see the wet stains from the dew laden grass on the toes of her boots. She walks this path so often that she hasn't bothered to turn on any lights. *Why didn't I make an paved path to the barn?* she thinks as the dampness soaks through her boots and makes her toes curl away from the cold. She tugs the old jean jacket tighter around her chest and shivers. It is her favorite time of day to ride in the summer, before the desert sun blasts all energy out of the day. But it is only April, the sun has not yet risen, and she is cold. She reaches the wrought iron gate in the block fence and pushes it open with a complaining groan from the hinges. *Gotta get Manuel to oil the hinges*, she thinks. The motion sensor turns the light on as she enters the barn yard. She is momentarily blinded by the bright lights and slows her steps. She can hear the soft snoring of horses, some muffled stirring from within the barn, and the sharp crack of a hoof stomped on the hard ground. She knows she will be waking the animals when she goes inside and they will all want some attention, so she stops, turns her back to the light, looks up, and savors the quiet calm, and the vast starlit sky that shows no hint of sunrise yet.

She slips through the side door of the barn and flicks on a single switch. The breezeway comes alive as the shadows flee. Moths, that must have been waiting in the rafters, are already swarming around the lights, hitting the bulbs with sharp pops. Jesse, the big mutt who lives in the barn, approaches her, blinking sleep away. His walk is stiff legged and the hair on his back is standing upright. His lips are curled to show his teeth and she can hear the low rumble of his growl.

"It's me, Jesse," she whispers, crouching and looking at the ground in front of the dog to avoid eye contact. Jesse weighed in at a lean 115 pounds at the last vet visit and he takes his job as barn protector seriously. She is not about to offer the dog any sort of threat. The dog's lips droop to cover his teeth, the hair on his back flattens, his growl turns to a high pitched whine, he drops his head, and his ears flatten as he recognizes her. She stands slowly, ruffles his heavy coat, and scratches behind his ears as he fawns at her feet. He leans against her hip, escorting her down the alley of the barn, bouncing like a playful puppy.

Her horse, Jamila, pokes her head over the door of her stall. The woman marvels, once again, at the innate beauty of the animal. The horse squints her big brown eyes and blinks rapidly at the insult of the light, her nostrils flare to catch the scent of the intruder, and she nickers when the woman walks up to the stall. Cold air blows in from Jamila's outside door. The door is open as the mare hates to be confined and will kick the barn walls in her attempts to get outside if locked in.

"Ready for an early morning ride?" the woman asks reaching up the scratch the young horse's forehead. The mare nods her head as if agreeing and the woman chuckles. A cloak of sadness drapes her like a shawl as she thinks of never seeing her horses or riding again and she allows herself a moment of self-pity. She shakes it off and throws each horse a small amount of hay to appease them until Manuel comes to feed them later this morning. The woman has to turn on another light and she too has a moment of blinking adjustment to the bright lights in the tack room. She hooks a plain, one ear bridle over the saddle horn and hitches her old saddle onto her hip to carry to Jamila's stall. She'll saddle the horse in her stall and let the mare munch on her hay until they leave so Jamila won't miss breakfast too badly.

It takes a supreme effort to lift the saddle onto Jamila's back despite the mare's petite size. The woman's arms scream in pain and she has to wait a moment before she can attempt to tighten the girth. Jamila expands her ribcage and abdominal muscles to extend her belly and keep the girth loose. The woman sighs in exasperation.

"Today," she says to the mare, "I don't even care." She scratches along the horse's mane as she slides her arm up the horse's neck. With her hand between the horse's ears, she pulls the bridle up, slips the bit in Jamila's mouth, and pulls the headstall over the mare's ears in one practiced move. The pair slip out of the stall, down the alley, and the woman switches the lights off. As she leads the horse out toward the dark barnyard, Jamila throws her head and pulls back away from the empty darkness. The woman has to keep talking and scratching the horse's neck to keep her moving away from the comfort of the stall. Jamila tosses her head up and away as the woman flings a rein over the far side of the horse's neck, then the horse sidles sideways as the woman tries to put her foot in the hanging stirrup. There are no motion sensor lights here and the woman has to mount by feel and experience.

"Jamila," the woman speaks softly. *"Solamente*

3

yo, mija. We're just going up the hill and you love to go up the pass and watch the sun rise."

Okay, she thinks, *I like to watch the sun rise on Overton Pass. But you need your little butt worked.* This thought creates the flow of sadness again as the woman realizes that she doesn't have much time to make this horse into the ride that Josh wants. Josh is a good rider, but without her patience and experience, she worries that he is too impetuous for this Arabian mare. But he wants her for his own. The saddle slips to the side from the weight of the woman swinging onto the horse's back. She pushes hard on the right stirrup to straighten it when she has alighted into the seat of the saddle, loosening her hips to flow with the horse already in motion. Their passage catches the sensor and the barnyard light springs to life causing the mare to hop sideways, nearly unseating her rider. The horse prances all the way to the property gate. As the woman leans down to fumble through the combination of the lock on the gate, she is impressed that the mare stands quietly. The barn light stays on just long enough for her to work the combination, then the pair is enveloped in early morning darkness and blinded by having been in the light. As her eyes adjust to the lack of barn light, the woman looks up from her task. She realizes that she can clearly see the outlines of the trail, and the sky fading to blue, causing the weaker stars to fade out. When the lock is released from its station, the mare sidles her body away from the gate. The horse grabs the latch in her teeth and opens the gate.

"Probably not a good thing to let you do," the woman says, pushing hard on the left stirrup to put the saddle back in the center of the horse's back. "But, what the hell, I'm not gettin' off." The mare pushes the gate wide with a shove of her nose and the pair is out on the open desert.

I should close that gate, the woman thinks. She tries to turn the horse around to do so, but the cold early morning air has infused her horse with tense energy. The woman forgets about the gate, concentrating on staying in the saddle, and going where she intends.

The rising sun creates a halo of sickly green revealing the outline of the foothills ahead of them. The woman sits firmly in the saddle, holding tightly to the reins, the braided leather catching the skin between her little and ring fingers. The sunrise should be to her right, but the mare performs a perfect sidepass on the trail, and they are looking directly at the foothills to the east. The rider watches the cholla they pass, that are too close to the horse's legs and tail. She worries what will happen if they brush one. The slightest brush of even the horse's tail will cause the cactus to loose its barbed spines and "shoot" either spines or a whole pod of spines. Once embedded in skin the barbed cholla needles hurt like hell and are hard to remove. The woman knows that this horse will go berserk if one spine attaches itself anywhere. She thinks about how much easier it would be to have taken one of the other horses out on this foray.

"Jamila, *te amo*," the leather saddle creaks as the woman leans forward and whispers to the mare's ears that alternately flick backward to catch every word. "You know this trail like you know your stall," she continues. "Don't be afraid, *mija.*"

Holding the reins tightly in one hand, the rider reaches up to scratch the arched neck of her tense horse. Jamila turns to follow the trail and the rider risks a moment of inattention to the mare to breathe in the view of her beloved desert foothills. It is light enough for the woman to see the saguaro cacti standing sentinel on the sides of the foothills surrounding her, though they throw no shadows yet. The urine soaked cedar scent of damp sage is potent perfume and she breathes it in deeply.

5

Roadrunners dart for cover from the approaching horse and rider and a covey of Gambel's quail bob from a jojoba bush to a prickly pear cactus at the edge of the trail. The rider watches as the male quail leads his brood to the edge of the trail and checks it before allowing the ten fuzzy chicks to cross. Mom quail chirps from behind, keeping them together, as they bobble across the trail ahead. The woman smiles at the picture of family unity.

She revels in fact that she owns all of this land bordering the county park. She overpaid for much of the property, but she could afford it once her books had become best sellers. Living "back east" had been exciting for a while with the hustle and bustle and the celebrity life, but she dreamed for years of returning to this area she loves. She tore down houses and barns she bought to recreate the pristine desert she had ridden for many years prior to moving east. The current sight thrills her. She turns in the saddle to take in the view of her little oasis. The three houses and the barn clustered in a small area and the rest of the land left to return to natural desert. The entire property is fenced to keep out joggers, bicyclists, and quad riders to protect the natural beauty.

She chooses Overton trail this morning as it offers a sustained incline that gives the horse good exercise and requires that a young horse learn to watch where it is going to avoid tripping. Jamila, at the age of six, is still flighty and prone to inattention, as some Arabian horses are, but the rider loves the challenge of this often unpredictable breed. A tear streaks the rider's cheek as she remembers her beloved Gatsby, the first of her Arabs she had taken on this trail. Gatsby is dead for many years now, before she moved east, but she still misses him. She released his ashes to the breeze at the top of this pass the day before she left for New York. It seemed the right thing to do since he seemed to love these desert trails as much as she still does.

The rider continues to talk nonsense to the her nervous horse and this finally achieves the desired effect. Jamila's hooves begin to stay on the ground longer and dance less. The horse stretches out her neck and lowers her head, pulling at the bit so that she can see the ground she is covering. Jamila finally stops swinging her head from side to side searching for the bogeyman to jump out from the surrounding cacti. The rider eases the reins through her fingers slightly so that the horse can focus on the rocky trail. Despite the fact that the saddle slipped back when they started on the incline, both horse and rider are relaxed and enjoying their early morning ride.

The sun has almost topped the mountain when the pair start their ascent of Overton Pass trail. There is still a cool mist hanging in the early morning air. Some of the deeper crevasses actually have small patches of fog obscuring them. The breeze that follows them is cool, but with a promise of warmth to follow.

The woman reaches into her jacket pocket and pulls out a nearly new pack of cigarettes. She is careful to maintain her grip on the reins as she pulls a cigarette out of the pack, puts it in her mouth, and tries to light a match. It has been many years since she quit smoking and she is unpracticed in the art of lighting a cigarette on horseback. The second match gets the cigarette lit and the woman inhales deeply. In a moment she is lightheaded and euphoric and she embraces the long lost feeling. With the cigarette and reins in one hand, she reaches down to scratch the horse's neck again. She inhales deeply on the cigarette and wonders which is better: the taste and feeling the tobacco gives her or the heady, pungent scent of the clean, cool, early morning desert air. She is pondering this idea and drops the cigarette from lax fingers when Jamila suddenly hops over a crack in the trail. The woman turns to see where the burning cigarette fell and prays that there is nothing there to start a fire.

Tiny hedgehog cacti hide under an ironwood tree only to proclaim their presence by the bright fuchsia flowers on their tops. Prickly pear cacti growing on the sides of the trail bear red fruit in contrast to the flat grey-green pads of the plant. Jamila drops her head so that her velvet nose is almost to the ground as the trail narrows and becomes steeper. The woman eases more of the reins through her fingers so that the horse can watch her footing freely. The flora on the ascent decreases as the numbers of boulders increase. They pass a small ironwood clinging to the side of the trail where the rugged, rock and cactus strewn land drops off to a deep crevasse between the two foothills. The drop is about thirty feet, nearly straight down. Rocks, jarred loose by the passing horse, tumble down the side of the hill, creating an uneven drumbeat in their descent. A cactus wren chastises them for disturbing her morning then glides away quickly. This is an area the rider often gets nervous as the trail is only wide enough for one horse and a slight mistake can be deadly. The right side of the trial is nearly as steep as the left but reaches up into the lightening blue sky. A huge, flat boulder juts out from the right constricting the trail. Horse and rider round a bend in the trail and can now see the top of the foothill with morning light working its way there. A pale moon hangs over the hills, desperately clinging to its position, until the bright desert sun will blot it out of the sky.

It is at this point that a coyote slinks onto the trail from behind a boulder. He stops in the middle of the trail looking directly at horse and rider. His tongue hangs out and he bares his teeth in a wicked grin. The woman sees the coyote when he slinks from behind the boulder and the horse notices him immediately afterward. The horse's explosive reaction is too sudden for the woman to prepare for. Jamila emits a shriek, flares her nostrils at the scent of a hunter, and twists her body in a "U" to escape. The motion is unchecked due to the loose reins. The horse's nostrils flare bright red, her eyes so wide the white sclera shows clearly. One slender rear leg slips off the trail, sinking into the dirt and loose rocks on the side, sending an avalanche of rocks and dirt down the hill. The horse lunges to throw itself down the trail to the safety of home. The saddle slips to the side with the violent motion of the horse's lunge. The woman finds herself dangling from the side of her mount directly over the rocky crevasse. The woman, unable to regain her balance after the horse's initial spin, sails head first into the canyon. The reins slip easily through slack hands. She doesn't make a sound until the impact with the rocks knock the breath out of her with a "hhmmph." Her head slams onto the rock that will serve as her final pillow. The coyote yips sharply, and Jamila bolts for home. The horse's ears lay flat against her head, nostrils flared in a nose pointed toward home. Mane and tail whip like flags in hurricane winds. The coyote hops onto the flat boulder to gain a vantage point and watch the devastation he created. He sits down, raises his head to the fading moon, and howls, then watches placidly as the horse races down the trail at a suicidal rate. The saddle, hanging under horse's belly, threatens to trip the horse with every step until the girth snaps and the saddle tumbles down the ravine. Lost in the low growing cacti, rocks, and dust. At the bottom of the hill, when the land flattens, Jamila tosses her head and the bridle flies to rest among the cholla lining the trail. Red dust devils swirl marking the horse's direction and the coyote watches intently as if to gauge her progress. When the horse is out of sight the coyote rises and moves cautiously toward the opposite side of the trail where the woman is resting, but his ears twitch and movement halts when he detects noises from down the trail. He returns to the boulder to await the next opportunity for chaos.

2

Runner

Mark Sullivan glances at his watch as he raises his arm to wipe the sweat dripping into his eyes. It is still early enough that the air is cool, but Mark is sweating heavily from the effort of running up the trail. The trail, while not appearing steep when glancing at it from below, is actually quite a long incline. Mark's leg muscles bulge with the effort of the climb and his heart has reached its peak performance rate. His focus is down on the rocky and narrowing trail directly in front of him so it takes a moment for his brain to register that his peripheral vision has caught movement to his right. The sight of the coyote grinning at him from the flat rock causes his heart to lurch and his forward progress to come to an abrupt halt. Mark's heart races even faster, but not from exertion, and bumps raise along the flesh of his arms as he stares at the coyote staring at him. The coyote emits a tiny yip, clamps its mouth shut, and turns to meld into the desert landscape as if he is only an apparition. The coyote is out of sight before Mark realizes there is something odd on the other side of the trail. The side that drops off suddenly for about thirty feet with only

10

boulders, jojoba, and a few cacti clinging to the edge. Mark has been staying away from that side of the trail to avoid having a serious accident.

Shaking off the sight of the coyote grinning at him, he forces himself to look to the side of trail opposite where the coyote sat. He can clearly see the bottoms of a pair of boots. In a flash his mind registers that the boots have to be attached to a body as they are unsupported by any of the local flora or rock formations and pointing almost straight up into the air. Mark runs with the last of his energy to the edge of the cliff. Several rocks tumble into the void, bouncing off boulders on their way to the bottom. He finds a woman dangling, head down, over the steep, rocky edge. Her arms hang limply over her head. Jacket and t-shirt pulled by gravity revealing her midriff. She is held in position by the prickly pear cactus that grasps her hips and thighs. He kneels on the rough ground, sharp pebbles digging into his exposed knees, and reaches down to grab her legs above the boots. With a Herculean effort Mark pulls her up onto the trail. He checks for breathing then pinches her nose, tilts her head to open her mouth, and breathes into the oral cavity several times. He checks the neck for a pulse and, finding none, he punches hard on the woman's chest. Mark is an emergency room intern and knows full well what he is doing. He watches the chest rise from the next breath he forces into the oral cavity and feels the heart flutter a few times after forcible compressions on her chest.

A man arrives, drops his mountain bike, throws his helmet onto the rocks, and runs to Mark and the body. Another runner stops to watch Mark's efforts, his face almost as ashen as the body lying on the ground, but unable to take his eyes off the scene. Mark continues resuscitation efforts, instructing the biker to assist him. A group of riders on horseback chance upon the scene. The two trail leaders jump off of their horses and join the

11

group around the prone woman.

For a few short seconds, the woman's heart beats erratically giving Mark the incentive to keep trying to revive her. Then it stops again. Frustration and training drive him in persisting to save her.

"I don' think it's gonna work," drawls one of the cowboys, pointing his brown weathered hand toward the woman's head. His long, thick, saliva stained handlebar mustache adds more droop to his face than even the realization that he is seeing death can. He takes his weathered, sweat stained hat off, and holds it over his heart as he wipes his face and bald pate with a bandanna. A wad of tobacco shoots from his pursed mouth to land with a plop in the dust. "Don't think I ever seen anyone survive a wound like that 'un."

Mark stops pushing on the woman's chest and takes in the whole picture of the body he's been desperately trying to revive. His chest compressions have caused the head to turn slightly to the side and Mark can now see the deficit in the skull. He turns her face further to the side and can easily see a hole the size of a baseball in the back of the skull. Her hair hangs in clumps from the drying blood, dirt, and small rocks clinging to it. Mark gently places her head back on the dusty trail and starts to stand when he hears the coyote howl. His whole body shakes and bumps rise on his arms and back as if from a chill. He stands with a groan looking into the vast array of foothills as if he can find the perpetrator.

"Cancer o' this land," says the cowboy squinting in the direction of the howl and spitting another wad of tobacco on the ground .

Mark's adrenaline is still at an extreme high, but his body is worn out. He slumps to sit on the boulder that the coyote recently vacated. With a sigh he automatically starts stretching to ease the aches in his muscles. He looks up at the other men watching him. "I had to try." The other men nod in agreement.

The cowboy turns on his worn, dusty boots to his partner. He still holds his hat over his heart. He stuffed his bandanna into the rear pocket of his jeans where the circular outline of a tobacco can has been worn into the material. The two cowboys converse quietly for a moment. The second cowboy returns to the group of riders and horses, his chaps dragging in the dust, and spurs making straight cuts in the trail. As he approaches the group, one of the riders unties a sweatshirt from his waist and hands it to the wrangler. The wrangler mounts with the ease of practice, rides his horse to Mark, and hands him the sweatshirt. The look that passes between the two men speaks louder than words.

"I called 9-1-1," says the mountain biker. He is looking at Mark with a shared sadness. "She said someone would be here in a few minutes."

Mark just nods at the man. The sweat is drying on him almost instantly in the dry desert morning. He dons the welcome sweatshirt and covers his face with his hands. Mark scrubs at his eyes, his shoulders rolled in defeat, his head hanging low.

By the time the police arrive on quads, Mark is standing guard over the body he found while continuing with routine stretches. The riders turned their horses around to seek a different trail for their morning ride, leaving only the cowboy leader, and the mountain bike rider to stay with Mark. The ashen-faced runner had vomited profusely when Mark turned the woman's head to examine the skull. The young man slunk down the trail at a shambling walk, dry heaving repeatedly. The three on the hill heard a car engine start up then tires squealing on pavement in the still morning.

The police survey the area, putting stakes into the unwieldy ground. They wind yellow warning tape around the tops of the stakes, to block the area from further curious tramping. It is an effort in futility since, if this is a crime scene, many people, horses, and bikes have left their marks on the dusty trail. Mark and the others have traversed the area leaving their footprints and obscuring any evidence that may have been present before Mark found the body. And Mark moved the body from its original position in his efforts to revive it.

A young, smooth faced officer approaches Mark. "You're the one who found the body?" The young man is trying to be officious, squaring his narrow shoulders, and standing as tall as he can. Mark feels ancient and huge next to this officer. Silently Marks bets himself that the kid doesn't shave more than twice a week.

When Mark nods his assent, the young officer leads him off the trail to the rocky escarpment previously occupied by the coyote. Mark answers all of the questions as best he can. He did not see anyone else until the mountain biker came along. The body was still warm and flexible so she had apparently just died, or was still dying, when he pulled her up from the edge of the cliff. Mark tries his best to show the young officer exactly where he found the body, but he had been so focused on his run and then trying to save the woman, that he can't remember. Besides, now he is exhausted, dirty, and defeated. He doesn't like to lose a patient, even if she was probably dead when he found her.

The sun is now high enough in the sky that the sweatshirt is too warm for Mark. He shrugs out of it, folding it neatly. He steps down the trail toward the cowboy who brought him the sweatshirt. The cowboy is still holding his hat over his heart and talking to an older, taller, and huskier version of the young man questioning

Mark. The skinny, young officer grabs Mark's arm with serious intent as Mark tries to return the sweatshirt.

"Just a minute," the kid says. "I'm not through here." He is still trying to sound more important than he looks and Mark lets frustration and anger take hold of him.

"I just wanna return the damn jacket," he says roughly pulling his arm out of the officer's grip. "I'm not gonna run away."

The officer backs away from Mark and unconsciously places his hand on the butt of his holstered gun. "Oh," he stammers, "okay." He squares his shoulders and flexes his arms as if trying to fill out the loose fitting uniform.

"Am I a suspect or sumthin'?" Mark asks. This comment loud enough to attract the attention of the older, presumably more experienced, officers in attendance. One of the older officers approaches Mark and the young rookie, his cowboy boots slipping on the loose rocks.

"Look," continues Mark in a calmer tone seeing trepidation on the young man's face and noting the hand on the gun. "I've told ya everything I know. I need to go home, shower, and get to work." He glances at his watch for emphasis. When he looks up, the older officers is standing next to the rookie, a big hand over the young man's hand on the gun.

The more mature officer looks patiently at Mark. "Sorry, but sometimes these things take too long." The older officer pulls a small, brown, plastic covered notebook from the breast pocket of his fitted tan shirt. He reaches his right hand out to Mark in a gesture of friendship, his left hand surreptitiously taking the young officer's hand off the gun butt. "Officer Woolrich," he says, "Just gimme your name, phone number, work number, cell, whatever. So we can reach you if we need to ask anything more, okay? Then we'll get ya goin' on your way."

Mark gives him the information and is walking down the slope in short order. As he treks down the trail, he turns to view the scene behind him. He sees the woman's body being zipped into a body bag. He can hear the older officer speaking to the rookie, turning and gesturing with apparent instructions, as the rookie eagerly nods. Mark can't understand anything he says beyond the statement, "This'll be your case, Roger, but..."

God help her, thinks Mark.

3

SEAN

"Mom?" his teenage voice cracks from raging hormones as he pushes open the heavy wood door and peers into the shadowy entryway. Sean jumps, then blushes at his foolishness, as the door bumps the doorstop and echoes hollowly against the walls. *This is my house,* he thinks, *what am I afraid of?* He steps into the Saltillo tiled entry way, his sneakers squeaking on the tiles. "M-O-M!" his voice echoes off the vaulted ceiling. He closes the door with a dull thud and walks past the sunken living room. The black cat jumps off one of the chairs, trots over to him, and winds between his feet, purring, and nearly tripping him as he walks further into the house. He peeks around a corner, down the long hall that leads to her office and his room. He half expects his mom to pop out of one of the rooms and greet him. She sometimes plays those kinds of games with him; ignoring his calls only to jump out of a shadow to startle him. *Like playing peek-a-boo with a baby,* he thinks. He snorts at the thought, but a slight smile raises the corners of his mouth.

"MOM," he yells louder than before, continuing to walk through the house. "Where's Mom?" he asks the feline reaching up his pant leg with outstretched paws, claws digging into his thigh. The cat follows him, purring audibly, and meowing questions at him. He peers into the laundry room and surveys the closed washer and dryer, the closed cabinets, and no clothes piled waiting to be cleaned. Not a total surprise since he hasn't been home for a few days. A quick glance into the workout room reveals the same unused look of neatness, so he turns back the way he came. He gathers the cat into his arms and she settles on his shoulder, nuzzling his ear. In the kitchen he glances out the windows into the lush back yard. Beyond the stucco and brick fence enclosing the yard he can see the horse pastures and barn. Manuel's shabby straw hat bobs like an injured bird over the top of the fence that separates the yard from the horse pastures. All of the horses are lounging under the corrugated aluminum shade munching their afternoon hay. Three dogs are lined up along the block fence, in the shade, enjoying the cool. They haven't seen or heard him yet or they would be running to the house to greet him. The pool sparkles invitingly, like sequins on a dancer's gown, in the spring sunlight and he squints from the brightness. Mom is not lounging in one of the chairs by the pool or pulling weeds from one of her many planting areas. He turns back to the kitchen scratching his head at the nagging thought that won't materialize. He opens the refrigerator, glances guiltily around the house, grabs the milk carton, and takes a long swig.

Mom would kill me if she saw me, he thinks and grins mischievously.

He scans the back yard, again, leaning over the gleaming sink to get a complete view. He takes out a glass and pours some milk into it. *If she was out there the dogs would be at her heels*, he thinks. He starts opening cabinet doors, looking for the right snack, an

18

unconscious, worried frown creasing his young forehead. Between each cabinet door he opens, he glances into the yard, just in case his mom suddenly appears. Inside the pantry door he spies her calendar filled, as usual, with notes and appointments. He notes that she has Consuelo's name written in for cleaning tomorrow. He bites his lip knowing that this should concern him, but not able to grasp the reason. Nothing written in for today but a Dr. Sands appointment on the day he left to stay with Dad. For a fleeting moment he tries to remember who Dr. Sands is but it's not interesting enough to maintain his attention. Finding the snack he wants, he wanders into the living room. He plops into a soft, deeply padded chair, draping his leg over the arm of the chair, and turns on the television. Despite the comfort, he jumps up in a moment, and resumes wandering through the house.

"Mom," he says quietly tiptoeing into her office. This is restricted territory. He glances over his shoulder again to be sure Mom isn't spying from some hidden vantage point trying to catch him. He turns back to the office and sees a rare sight. The desktop reflects the light due to its recent polishing. No papers are scattered, the computer is hidden away in its compartment, the desk drawers and file cabinets are all closed, and presumably locked. The multitude of books lining the shelved walls are all neat and dust free. "Mom," he calls a little louder.

"She musta finished her book and gone out, hey Muse?" he asks the big tabby cat occupying the deep window ledge of the office. The cat blinks lazily and yawns at him in response. He opens the center drawer of the desk and pushes aside some pens and papers searching for something. Muse jumps on the desk and reaches his paw into the drawer to bat at the boy's hand. It's as if the cat wants stop Sean from searching the drawer. Sean doesn't know what he is looking for, but he feels the discomfort of guilt crawling up his back. He shrugs his narrow shoulders to dispel the feeling. As he closes the drawer and looks up, he catches sight of the phone sitting suggestively at the top corner of the big desk. It is the phone to his mom's private line, the one that his friends don't call him on. He grabs the handset and scoots out of the office. He feels lighter as soon as he clears the doorway to that room. Consuelo doesn't even go in there to clean.

Sean heads back to the living room, grabbing the snack bag he left on the breakfast table as he passes. He falls into a chair and puts the snack bag next to him, within easy reach. He punches some numbers on the phone, shakes his head and stuffs the phone between the seat cushion and arm of the chair.

When the second episode of "Sponge Bob Square Pants" ends, he grabs the phone again and absently hits the speed dial. He needs to talk to someone; it is too quiet in the house. The cats have deserted him and sought sunny places to relax so he feels quite alone.

"Hey, bro'," he smiles at his oldest brother's response. It has been a while since they've talked, so they catch up on their individual schools, local sports, and current girlfriends for a while. Sean does the usual teasing by asking Mike how the weather is in Vermont. Living in the sunbelt has its advantages in the winter and early spring. He can hear the smile in Mike's voice when Mike responds and it makes Sean smile, too.

"Have you heard from Mom today?" Sean's voice squeaks again. He blushes despite the fact that his brother is nearly three thousand miles away and wouldn't tease him about something over which he has no control.

He surfs through the channels listening to the response. "Well," he replies after a pause, "ya know I'm staying with Dad while he's here for spring break. I stopped home to get some clean clothes and see Mom and she's not here. The house is empty," he looks around the spacious interior of the house, "and clean." He finally settles on watching the Suns-Seattle game, then responds, "Yeah, well, we both know she only cleans the house when she's finished a project, so I thought maybe she mighta told ya 'bout it." He frowns while listening to his brother. "She didn't tell me about any plans when I talked to her yesterday. Consuelo's due out tomorrow but the house is spotless." His voice pitches into a squeak but he fails to be embarrassed this time. He stares blankly at the television screen, a frown settling on his young forehead, as that niggling worry is trying to make itself known again. He distractedly responds to his brother's queries and they hang up with a promise to talk soon. He wanders about the house for a while then dials the phone again.

"Hey, Dad," his voice squeaks. "Can ya come pick me up? Mom's not here."

He listens for a minute then says, "I dunno, maybe she finished her book and is with her agent or somethin'." He listens again for a moment longer then punches the "End" button on the phone. As he walks the phone back to the office, he looks around the house and shivers. He feels cold despite the warmth of the house. He grabs his clean clothes, carefully closes the heavy front door, and begins the trek to meet his dad. It is a long walk to the front gate and Sean welcomes the warm sunshine on his shoulders.

4

MARICOPA COUNTY MORGUE

Roger Albright's footsteps echo off the gleaming green walls of the morgue. He stops near one of the stainless steel tables with a partially covered body on it. Staring intently at the ceiling, he reaches into the breast pocket of his uniform and pulls out a small notebook and a pen. Ralph Emerson, the medical examiner on duty, is standing on the opposite side of the table. The young officer adjusts his gun belt several times as if the weight is pulling the pants off his narrow hips.

"Any ID on the body?" Albright asks, staring intently at his notebook, as if it might answer his question. He tugs at his gun belt again.

"Nothing in the jacket or pants pockets," replies the middle aged man with a surgical mask muzzling most of his face and a gown of gauzy material covering his clothes. He pushes the clear plastic shield up from over his eyes and looks directly at the young officer. Albright twitches his shoulders, but doesn't return the gaze.

"She was wearing a worn, old jean jacket, Wrangler jeans, a white, long sleeved, cotton t-shirt, cotton socks, and cotton underwear. A pair of well worn Justin boots. Nothing in the pants pockets but 36 cents. The only jewelry was this necklace with a ring on it." He holds up a small plastic bag, and reaches over to the young officer to give it to him. The officer looks up only long enough to grab the bag then refocuses on his notebook, shrugging again.

"The ring is unusual. Looks like maybe it was custom-made. The only wear on the band is from the necklace it's hanging on. I'd guess it was never worn on a finger." Ralph leans back against the brushed stainless steel table behind him, sliding the surgical mask down his stubbly chin to his neck, and folds his arms across his chest.

"I found a pack of cigarettes, with an Arizona state stamp on the pack, in the pocket of the jacket. Only four cigarettes missing from the pack, so I would assume that she bought them shortly before she went out on the trail. A book of matches, with five matches missing, and several scratches on the lighter strip, a set of keys, house keys I'd say." The coroner reaches to the table behind him, and without looking hands the items to the officer. He leans toward the officer bracing himself with his thinly gloved hands on the table in front of him. He looks closely at the body lying there. The bright, surgical lights above reflect off the pale skin. The flaccid skin seemingly melting into the table top from the heat of the surgical lights. The blue eyes are open and staring blankly into the bright lights overhead.

"No vehicles found left in the area," sniffs the officer. The gleam of Vick's VapoRub glistens on his upper lip like nervous perspiration. He keeps his eyes averted from the body on the table.

"She musta come from one of the nearby houses." Roger glances up, immediately locking his view to the top of the bright lights shining on the body, and pushes the gun belt downward.

Cause of death, Ralph." Roger asks twitching his shoulders and dropping his eyes to the floor.

"First, you can call me Doctor Emerson," the medical examiner replies with calm indignation. Emerson lets this sink in for a moment, then continues. "In overview: I'd say a sharp blow to the occipital region of the skull. Damage to the skull and brain are consistent with the size and shape of rocks in the area where she was found." The medical examiner gently lifts the head and turns it to the side so Albright can easily view the damage to the skull. The hair hangs in blood-clotted clumps, shards of bone, red dirt, and small stones glued to the fist sized deficit of the skull.

"Looks to me like she fell from a height and hit her head on a rock. Possibly was riding a horse and was thrown or fell." Emerson gently places the head back on the gleaming table and brushes the hair that has fallen across the face away.

Albright is writing diligently in his notebook. "Body was moved by the hiker who found her. He tried to perform CPR until he realized it was useless and called 9-1-1 on his cell phone. Him and some other good Samaritans walked all over the area so there were no usable footprints." He pauses, but continues to page through his notebook. "Anything we can use for ID?" he sniffs.

Ralph Emerson turns to face the young officer. "Well, I can tell you a few things just from a cursory exam: she's about fifty, in pretty good physical shape, five foot six inches tall, 135 pounds, Caucasian, probably of western European descent, Irish or English I'd say." Ralph reaches under the gleaming table with the body on it and picks up a plastic bag, pillow shaped from the contents.

"From the looks of her clothes, she was out riding her horse." He pulls a pair of blue jeans out of the bag and releases a pungent, distinctive odor; the not unpleasant smell of horse sweat and feces, into the room. "The smell is pretty distinctive. There is brown staining to the inside of each pants leg. Consistent with what you would find on the jeans of a cowboy after a ride in a leather saddle. You need to find a horse that came home without its rider." He stuffs the jeans back into the bag and places the bag back under the table. "I sent prints and DNA to the lab, any results?"

The officer is writing in his notebook without looking up or at the body. He flips back a page and mumbles to the medical examiner, "No match on the prints. No criminal record." Albright's whole body twitches.

"I didn't think so," Ralph replies lowering his face to look directly at the body on the table. "You don't look like a criminal to me." He gently caresses the cadaver's cheek and pushes a stray lock of hair away from the forehead. Albright looks up in time to witness this action and a disgusted look crosses his face.

"We'll have to wait on the DNA for processing." Albright turns back to a blank page in his notebook. "Any distinguishing marks or scars?"

"Actually, shouldn't be too hard to identify this one." Ralph picks up a dead hand and gently places it on the sheet covering the lower half of the body. "She's got a lot of scars. Some surgical and fairly recent." The sheriff finally looks at the medical examiner with a glimmer of interest crossing his face.

"Want me to start at the top and work my way down?   Or start with what appear to be the most recent?" Emerson is watching the officer, his lips slightly curling up on one side of his mouth.   Albright is absorbed in his open notebook again and fails to notice the interest.

"Whatever you think is best." Albright replies without looking away from the notebook and shrugging again.

Doctor Emerson turns back to the body lying on the table with a shake of his head and a wry grin.

"Well, starting at the head: she has one deep scar, mid-line crown, not a new scar, several surrounding shallower scars, all aligned..."

5

FALL 1971

The big engine of the car roars evenly as the three young people contained inside it cruise down the highway. The rain beats a constant rhythm on the convertible top. They are traveling at or below the speed limit due to the rain-slicked highway. The atmosphere inside the car is festive as the radio thrums the new Simon and Garfunkle song, "Bridge Over Troubled Waters" just loudly enough to make the occupants of the car speak out.

"Did ya hear about Nicky and Paula?" the small, dark, young man in the back seat leans forward and inserts himself between the bucket seats. He looks with absolute seriousness from driver to front seat passenger. "They gotta get married now. Bambino on the way." Costa falls back into the back seat with a huff of expressed air and performs the sign of the cross. "Thank God my girlfriend is onna pill. I ain't gonna get caught that way."

Ronnie pulls his eyes off the road and glances at his girlfriend in the passenger seat. She smiles back at him with a knowing smile. Costa's dramatics are a constant source of amusement to them. Ronnie forces his eyes back to the road ahead and down-shifts to third gear as they approach a curve in the highway. The car's wide rear tires slip slightly on the rain slicked road. He thinks about how much he loves to look into those blue eyes and run his fingers through her long brown hair. He reaches into his jacket pocket and palms the small box hiding there. He'd invited Costa along tonight because he needed someone to distract her while he picked up the ring from the jewelers. He wants to surprise her with it later, when they are alone. The box contains an engagement ring. It is a simple ring with three small diamonds. "She'd designed it herself when drawing pictures one night. Ronnie smiles with anticipated delight then grips the steering wheel with both hands as the car slips again.

Costa returns to his perch between the couple in the front seats. He resumes his discussion about birth control and the parties coming up Ron's girlfriend settles back into the passenger seat smiling and nodding to Costa, but quietly singing along to the radio. Ron is driving in the left lane, despite the fact that he is driving slowly. There is less standing water on the roadway in the left lane. It's Friday night and there is traffic surrounding them. They have taken Ron's "new" street rod out for a spin. It's the car he dreamed of owning for the last few years and Ron wants to feel it run on the open road. The rain has dampened his desire to let it out and test the big engine, but he can feel the power anyway. The car is a challenge to his nineteen year old driving skills, but he enjoys the feel of potential under the hood.

The curve of the road rounds an overpass and Ron stares at the highway ahead. His view of the road is blocked by the overpass supports and he lets off the gas somewhat, not wanting to brush the guardrail.

"Oh my God," screams his girlfriend from the passenger seat. Ron steals a glance at her and when his eyes return to the road ahead he sees her concern: Headlights facing directly at them. Ron jams on the brakes, the car slides sideways, wide tires fighting to find purchase on the slick road. He glances to his right. There is a car next to him, a guardrail on the left, and his car isn't stopping.

"Shit," is the frantic whisper from the back seat, as the car slides, uncontrolled, toward the looming headlights.

The sounds of sheet metal ripping and glass shattering tear into the night as the two cars meet. Ron's girlfriend crosses her arms over her face and ducks her head. Ron braces himself with a stiff armed grip on the steering wheel, his right foot jamming the brake pedal to the floor. Costa tries to throw himself flat onto the back seat. The night encloses the two cars as the headlights are extinguished and the cars merge into one scrap pile. Moments later the car following Ron's creates a pile of three with more rending of sheet metal and shrieks from the cars being demolished.

Silence encases the interior of the little hot rod, except for the rain continuing its steady rhythm on the roof of the car.

Her first conscious thought is how cold her lower legs are. When she opens her eyes, she sees the rain dripping through the top of the windshield where it has popped out of its restraining frame. She thinks that something hard must have hit the windshield when she spies the bulging spider web of cracks directly in front of her. Slowly, she becomes aware of the fact that there are a lot of people surrounding the car. She can't remember where she is and looks to her left to see her beloved Ron slumped over the steering wheel, not moving.

She raises her head, wipes the warm moisture off her forehead, and turns to look again at Ron. Costa quietly gasps, then turns and kicks the driver's side door repeatedly until it budges open. With a groan and a screech of metal against metal, the door gives way enough for him to squeeze out of the car. He runs around to the passenger door, pushing the gawkers out of his way and wrenches open the door next to her.

"I'm a nurse. Can I take a look at her?" A stranger's voice comes from the group around the car. Costa backs away to let the woman minister to the young girl and he turns back to Ron. Several other cars pull off the highway and people get out, staring at the grotesque scene. One person is smart enough to light and put out flares up the highway where the road curves and the over pass support blocks the view of the accident.

"Oh my God," a woman in the crowd screeches. "Did anyone survive?" Costa glares at her from his squatting position next to Ron and several other people lead her away from the scene whispering admonishments. The nurse holds on to Ron's girlfriend's arm as she frantically pushes her way out of the car.

"I gotta get outta here. This thing's gonna blow up," she pants breathlessly staring wild eyed at the steam rising from what was the engine compartment. The nurse helps her out of the car, over the guardrail, and onto the median grass, away from the wreckage. They both look to see the flashing lights of a police car and ambulance arriving on the scene. The girl trembles violently in the' nurse's arms.

"Ron," the girl whispers, "Ronnie, where are you?" She tries frantically to reach the tangle of metal, but several people hold her back as the ambulance attendants and police officers carefully pull Ron from the car. He is pale and gasping for breath. She tears herself free from the grip of the strangers and runs to Ron. The ambulance attendants have placed him on the ground and run to the ambulance to retrieve the gurney. She leans over Ronnie, attempting to block the rain from hitting him, and looks into his eyes. When Ronnie sees her he smiles and struggles to reach into the pocket of his jacket.

"Will you marry me?" he gasps as the rain pours off of her head onto his pale face.

"Yes," she whispers, kissing him. The ambulance attendants gently push her aside and lift him onto a gurney. Before they can complete the trip to the back of the waiting ambulance, Ronnie extracts his hand from his pocket and reaches out to her. She grabs the small box from Ronnie's hand and Costa puts his arm around her as the attendants lift Ron in to the bright cave of the ambulance. Ron's face is obscured by the oxygen mask and the attendants scurry to secure the gurney and slam the ambulance doors closed.

"He'll be okay," says Costa without conviction. She collapses onto the wet grass, tears mingling with the rain washing her face as she watches Ron's ambulance scream away from the wreck.

The police have taken control of the scene and have many of the gawkers and their cars moving away. More ambulances arrive and the EMT's come over to check her out and look at the egg sized bump on Costa's forehead.

"We really need to take you both to the hospital," says one of the EMTs. "She's got quite a laceration on the top of her head and her knee is swollen. And you should have that bump looked at." Costa nods as he notices her glazed eyes, blood dripping down her face, and the fact that she is supporting herself on one leg. He reaches up to rub his forehead, but withdraws the hand at the stab of pain from the large lump he felt.

"Were any of you restrained by seatbelts?" asks the EMT. Costa can only shake his head in dismay. "Then you're lucky to be alive." The three look at the pile of scrap metal and glass that only minutes previously had been three cars.

Costa sits in the ambulance with her, talking the whole ride to the hospital. The siren's incessant scream causes her head to pound. She lies quietly letting the EMT's check and recheck her blood pressure, and gently swab the blood off of her face. One of the EMTs tries to wipe the blood away from the top of her head only to find shards of glass caught in her hair and scalp.

The hospital emergency room is a beehive of bustling activity and moaning, unhappy people. She is hustled into a curtained area where a young doctor shines lights into her eyes, examines her head, and makes her try to bend and straighten her left leg. She finally stops questioning him about Ron, when he tells her for the fourth time that he doesn't have any information. Shortly, a nurse pushes aside the curtain. She is carrying a stainless steel bowl and a lot of gauze sponges. The nurse sits at the top of the young girl's head and starts extracting shards of glass from her hair and scalp.

"Where's Ron?" she asks.

"They took him to surgery," the nurse answers quietly.

"Will he be okay," she asks clutching the small box he gave her before they were torn apart.

"This might hurt." The nurse says quietly before

she pulls out glass embedded in the girl's scalp. Clumps of three foot long hair are falling to the floor and into the stainless steel bowl with the glass shards.

"How're ya feeling, honey?" the nurse asks periodically. The girl continues to answer all questions put to her and the nurse visibly relaxes. Another nurse enters the room and pulls a pair of scissors out of the deep pocket of her white jacket.

"I'm going to have to cut your jeans off," the second nurse says matter-of-factly. The young girl sits up suddenly.

"No," she wails. Both nurses jump, as the patient has been so quiet and compliant. The girl lies back down on the bed and says quietly, "I finally got these to the point where they fit right and look good." The nurses look down at the faded, patched, and embroidered jeans the girl is wearing.

"Did you do this yourself?" the nurse asks pointing to an area of neat embroidery at the bell of the pants.

"Mm-hmm," the girl replies. "I did all the added work myself." The nurses smile at each other and the note of pride in the girl's voice. "This one's a replica of the stuffed elephant that Ron gave me for Christmas." The nurses' smiles fade.

"Well, I'm done up here," the nurse at her head says. "Let's see if we can get those pants off without ruining any of your artwork, okay?" She smiles down at the young girl in her care, but it is a sad smile.

The three struggle to gently remove the girl from her jeans. Her left knee is so swollen that the pants are stretched to their limits and the girl's knee is shrieking with pain each time she moves her leg. She holds her expressions of pain to sharp intakes of breath, gritting of teeth, and an occasional moan. She never takes her eyes off the scissors outlined in the pocket of the second nurse's jacket. And she never stops asking about Ronnie, but the nurses have no answers for her.

The girl falls back onto the bed with a sigh when they finally get the pants past her swollen knee. Beads of sweat glisten on her forehead and upper lip, and her hands are shaking as she closes her eyes. One of the nurses puts her jeans in a plastic bag and places it under the bed the girl is lying on.

"Can you find out how Ron is?" she asks the closest nurse. The two women look at each other over the girl's head.

"I'll check on him," the younger nurse says and the two women leave the girl alone.

When her strength returns, the girl reaches up to scratch an itch on the top of her head. What her fingers find is a painful laceration directly in the middle of her center part, and several smaller lacerations surrounding it. Her head is too painful to continue to probe so she brings her hand back to rest on her abdomen. Trailing from her hand is a clump of long brown hair. She reaches to the top of her head and gives a gentle tug to her hair. "Oh my God!" she shrieks as clumps of her hair entwine in her fingers and come away from her scalp.

The young intern pushes open the drawn curtain, his face lined with concern.

"What did you do?" The girl cries. "You cut my hair off!"

A smile plays at the corners of the intern's mouth,

34

but he struggles to maintain a serious face as he can see the girl is upset. "Actually, I think that when you hit the windshield with the top of your head, the glass sheared the hair off." He is actually smiling now. "You have a fairly large bald spot up there." His smile disappears when the girl's face crumples and tears start to fall. "Don't worry, it'll all grow back." He reaches out and pats her hand with the wad of hair clutched in it. The girl just nods through the tears.

"If it'll make you feel better, we don't need to put any stitches in it," he says compassionately, "so we won't have to shave any more of those locks than the windshield did."

The girl nods, reaches up to scratch a shard of windshield out of her scalp, and tenderly probe the bald spot on top of her head. With a sigh she closes her eyes and waits for the x-rays of her knee to be taken. She examines the clump of hair caught in her fingers and a tear slowly leaks out of the corner of her eye. Ron is always running his fingers through her hair, telling her how much he loves it. *It'll grow back*, she reminds herself.

"How's Ron?" she asks the retreating back of the intern. The intern keeps walking as if he has not heard her speak, although there is a noticeable falter in his footsteps when she asks the question. She is clutching the small box that Ron gave her before they took him away. She opens the box and gasps when she sees what is inside. She had drawn almost this exact ring several months ago during a period of jewelry designing she'd attempted. Ronnie had it copied almost exactly. She closes the box as tears blur her vision. She decides that she will never wear the ring until Ron can put it on her finger himself.

Her head hurts and she wants to sleep, but is too

agitated waiting for someone to inform her of Ron's condition.

Her chest constricts and her heart drums in her ears when Costa comes into the curtained area with a sad-faced priest.

6

MIKE

The ringing phone echoes through the house. Muse jumps on the desk from his window ledge perch and sniffs at the phone. He raises a paw and touches the phone with it as if he might try to answer the ringing. After the fourth ring the cat hears his owner's voice and he meows.

"I'm probably out doing research for a new book…" Mike looks at his cell phone and ends the call with the idea that he will call Mom later. He hopes that she will be home. Sean sounded weird about her not being at the hacienda. He pulls open the door to the math building and the wind howls at his back. Mike shivers as he thinks about how eerily it sounds like the coyotes that roam his Mom's vast property.

7

MARICOPA COUNTY MORGUE

"Then we go to her forehead, where I've found a small, circular indenting scar. I thought at first that it was a pox or acne scar, but I'm not sure. It's not symmetrical enough and there is only one. Usually you would expect at least a few scars from chicken pox or acne." Doctor Emerson pauses a moment, still looking at the face of the cadaver. "Under her left eye is a tiny scar, surgical repair, I think, but very old. Position is not quite right for a blepharoplasty, so I assume that it is a surgical repair of an injury."

8

SUMMER 1957

Her chubby, two year old legs can only carry her so fast and she struggles to keep up with the rest of them. The game of "army" is not much fun in bare feet, marching along a rocky dirt path. She has a splintery old wooden slat for a gun resting on her shoulder. She brings the stick down from her shoulder and digs the end into the ground in front of her. It seems to help her walk a little faster. Last week when they played army, Jimmy threw a missile (a rock really) and hit her in the forehead. She reaches her dirty, chubby, fingers to her forehead to feel the deep hole left there when the scab fell off this morning. The moment of inattention to her feet causes her to stub her toe on a protruding rock. She doesn't cry out. She is a soldier, after all, and she knows how soldiers act. Her uncle just came back from a Korean prison camp. But, she loses all sense of balance and falls forward. She lets go of her "gun," but it sticks in the dirt, and stands upright just long enough for her to fall onto it. When the wooden slat jabs sharply under her left eye, she finally lets out a scream. The entire entourage freezes at the sound.

Ronnie, who had been leading the troops, drops her pretty blonde sister from the perch on his back. He runs back to see what the problem is. The two year old looks up at him, blood streaming from her left eye. Ronnie squats down in front of her, and, forgetting that he's always told her that she was too heavy for him to carry, instructs her climb on his back. She wants to be thrilled that Ronnie is finally carrying her but her eye hurts too much. She watches the open space give way to a few houses, while she bounces on Ronnie's back. Her tears form a pink circle on the shoulder of his shirt. Ronnie unceremoniously drops her on the stoop of her house, tells her sister to let their mom know what happened, and he and his siblings run to their own house.

"M-M-M-O-O-O-M," her sister screams, "Mom. M-O-M," she repeats. It is difficult to tell who the injured party is, with her sister screaming so loudly. Mom appears at the door to see what the noise is all about. Gloria grabs on to Mom's skirt immediately, blubbering, whining, crying, and trying to talk all at once. Mom picks her up to calm her trying to get the story. Then she glances at her messy little two year old, holding a chubby hand over her left eye. Streaks of blood tinged tears running down that child's face and onto her t-shirt. Mom drops Gloria to the stoop and bends to pick up her injured child.

With the calm that only an experienced mother can display in the face of an emergency, Mom pries the chubby little hand from the toddler's left eye. Mom's only reaction is a sharp intake of breath.

"Go ask Frank if he can drive me to the emergency room." Mom speaks softly, but looks hard at the still crying, blonde standing on the stoop, clinging to her skirt. "Go. Now."

The little blonde emits another loud wail, and bursts into tears. Gloria then runs across the road to the neighbor's house. A blue station wagon screeches to a halt in the driveway moments later. Frank's wife hauls her bulk out of the passenger seat and the little blonde crawls out from beside her.

"Hop in," the woman says. "Frank'll take ya to the hospital and I'll stay with the other kids."

Mom cradles the toddler in her arms right into the ambulance bay of the emergency room. The signs clearly state that the area is for ambulances only, but Frank parks his car there anyway. Frank reaches across the seat and grabs the child from her mother's arms. He bursts through the automatic doors almost before they have a chance to open. From his embrace, the toddler watches the bright lights, tinged red from the blood in her left eye, skate by overhead. She is no longer crying, just sucking her thumb.

"Get this kid a doctor." Frank yells at the nurse behind the desk. The nurse makes feeble attempts to stop the big man, but he simply walks past her into an empty, curtained exam area. He gently places the toddler on the crisp white sheets of the bed and murmurs gentle words to her.

A young, bespectacled man in a long white jacket enters the curtained area with the flustered nurse at his heels. "I tried to stop him…" the nurse babbles.

"Go back to the desk and get me some information on this child," the doctor says to her. The nurse leaves with an impotent glare in Frank's direction. Frank doesn't notice, his eyes are only for the little girl on the bed before him.

The doctor carefully examines the wound under the

child's eye and pronounces that she will need stitches to close the wound.

"Make it pretty," says Frank quietly as the doctor turns to grab a stainless steel tray and load it with supplies he will need. The tension in the exam room is palpable and the doctor's hands shake slightly as Frank carefully observes each stitch placed under the baby's eye. It takes four tiny, neat stitches to close the wound.

9

MORGUE

"I almost missed these scars," Doctor Emerson says pushing the hair back from the dead woman's forehead. "Very neat, fairly new scars running through the hairline and down in front of the ears." He pushes the plastic shield up to his forehead. He pulls his glasses from their perch on the neck of his shirt to put them before his eyes. He leans very close to the body and searches through the hair carefully tracing an invisible line along the hairline and face. "Looks like this lady has had a facelift. It is expertly done and the scars are nearly indiscernible..."

10

1999

She rifles through the mail and notes with agitation the number of bills piling up. There is a legal size envelope in the pile of mail, but she has left that for last, She assumes it is another letter from her lawyer calling her to court with her ex-husband once again. When she has perused the pile of bills and thrown out the junk mail, she finally turns her attention to the large manila envelope. She rips it open without looking at the return address. At first the words on the papers confuse her and her forehead puckers in a frown. The packet is not from her lawyer. She sets the pile of papers down on the table to look for a return address on the envelope. Seagull Publishers is printed in the top left hand corner. Still unable to grasp the meaning of the envelope, she picks up the pile of papers again and starts to read with comprehension this time.

"We are pleased to inform you..." the letter starts. With a jolt, she realizes that this is not just another rejection letter. They have accepted her book for publishing. The pile of papers is contracts.

"WhooEEE," she screeches and tosses the papers into the air. Lucky barks and starts to run around her owner. Lucky doesn't know why, she only knows that her master is happy, so she is happy. The woman does an impromptu sock dance atop the scattered papers, still making shrieking noises and pumping her fists in the air.

Lucky joins her in the dance, tongue lolling, barking, and jumping in front of her owner. Suddenly the woman stops dancing. She needs to tell someone. She frantically searches for a phone. They are never on the chargers where they belong. She realizes that this is her own fault and smiles.

"They're publishing my book," she says verbalizing to the dog before she speaks the magic to someone else. The dog wags her tail and bounces to her master's joy. But the woman is not satisfied, she needs to talk to a human being.

The kids are in school, she thinks. Cheryl is at work, and she gets everyone else's voice mail, and doesn't leave a message. She wants to shout the words to a friendly ear, not a machine. She rushes to the bathroom and looks in the mirror. The sight dampens her mood momentarily. All the years of fighting with her ex over the boys and smoking have taken their toll. She sighs at the dark circles under her eyes, the sagging jaw line and the wrinkles that yesterday meant nothing. But even this view cannot dampen her spirits for long.

"I'm being published," she shouts at her reflection. "My book is being published." The smile that reflects back makes her forget the lines and wrinkles and sags and bags of her face. All the years of writing stories and receiving only rejection letters for her effort fade into the background. Perusing the papers more carefully, she finds a statement for an advance toward the sales of her book.

It is enough to pull her out of the pits of debt and leave enough for some leisure activities. She sinks into the worn old couch and starts to make more phone calls. First to her sister, a lawyer and some more distant friends.

The months ahead are a whirlwind of contract signing, editing and rewrites. Phone calls from her new editor, legal investigations into the credibility of the book. And phone call upon phone call to and from friends. It is the most exciting period of her life. She hardly even notices when the letter arrives from her lawyer letting her know that her ex is taking her to court again. He is, of course, asking for a reduction in his child support due to her sudden increase in income. The book isn't even on the market yet, but he wants "his" share.

After months of preparation, the book finally comes out. She takes the boys to the local book store and the four of them stand in awe looking at the stacks of her story. Hard cover books with dust jackets and a colorful picture of the desert on the front. Mike is the first to pick up one of the books. He holds it in his hand reverently, almost as if weighing it. Slowly he turns the book over and his brothers look around his shoulders to see the picture of their mom gracing the back of the dust jacket. There is a short biography about her below the picture.

"Hey, Mom," Sean says. "It talks about us, too."

His brothers roll their eyes at their little brother's stupidity. They knew that they would be mentioned in some way. Mom always said she was writing her stories for them.

They watch as several people pick up copies of her book and peruse the inside. She has yet to pick up one of the books and look at it. She is frozen with awe at the sight of her name on the cover of a real book. She is afraid to move in case reality sets in and makes it disappear.

One of the men who picked up a book, suddenly looks at her with intense surprise. He is looking at the photo on the back of the dust jacket, then up at her. She is suddenly embarrassed and sorry that she had not taken more care with her appearance before they left the house. The man with her book in his hand starts to walk around the carousel approaching the foursome. Mike walks to stand between the man and his mom.

"This is you," the young man says to her holding the book out with her picture on the dust jacket staring her in the face. She is pleasantly surprised at how good the picture looks. It is just out of focus enough that she looks much younger. She nods to the young man.

"Will you sign this for me?" he asks thrusting the book at her.

"I... I don't..." she stammers with incredulity at the idea of someone wanting her to sign a book for them.

"Have a pen?" the young man finishes what he thinks she was going to say and makes a display of searching his pockets.

Their presence at the book display has drawn a few more people. The store manager notices and comes over the find out what the chaos is about. He seems pleasantly surprised to recognize her from her photo on the book.

"I am sure that after you purchase the books," the store manager announces loudly. "She would be happy to sign them for you." The manager looks at her for approval and she nods slightly. "I'll set up a table right over here past the cash registers." He turns away from her and the people surrounding her and directs some employees to set up a table and chair for her just past the registers.

Her legs are shaking and she drops into the chair behind the table. There are a few people standing and waiting for her. She opens the book to a blank page and stares at it, not knowing what to write.

"Ask him his name," Mike whispers in her ear, but she doesn't have to ask as the young man informs her at that moment. She tries to think of something creative to write, but her mind is blank.

She is about the sign the third book when Josh sighs loudly and leaves the group around the table. She watches him walk upstairs to the music department wishing he would stay with her. Sean, her youngest, is dancing excitedly around the table talking to the people waiting in line. She starts to write on the blank page of the book in front of her when her cell phone rings.

Mike reaches into her jacket pocket and grabs her cell phone. He looks at the caller's number and answers the phone. She vaguely hears him describing the scene that is ensuing. When she finishes with the book she was signing, Mike mouths the words "your agent" and smiles. He talks for a while longer, then hands the phone to the store manager who is hovering nearby.

The manager talks on the phone for a while, flips it closed and hands the phone back to Mike.

The astute store manager has had chairs brought for Mike and Sean and her two sons flank her as she signs a few more books. Another store employee brings a cup of coffee and two bottles of water. Mike grabs the coffee and she drinks from a water bottle between signings. She scans the upper level balcony to locate Josh, but she can no longer see him. He is wont to put on head phones and listen to the music that is available so she assumes that is where he is.

After an hour of the signing books, her hand is aching. She stops to stretch her fingers and massage the painful appendage. Mike watches this action with concern etching his young face. He gets up and leaves the table.

She is signing a book when the store manager comes to the table with Mike and announces loudly, "That will be all for the book signing," he says. "She'll be back here in two weeks for a scheduled book signing. Anyone who bought a book is welcome to come back then and have it signed."

The manager looks at her, gives her a wink, smiles at Mike and pats him on the shoulder..

She rises to stretch and once again scan the upper balcony for Josh. Several people are walking past with copies of her book in their hands. She overhears one couple discussing how much younger she appears in the picture than in real life and she blushes.

Surprisingly, to her, the book is a huge success. The reviews are mostly favorable and she finds herself scheduled for more book signings. She tries to schedule them when the boys are with her ex-husband so as not to upset Josh again. The local readings and signings lead to more distant visits and she and the boys often end up in places they would never have otherwise seen. Only Sean accompanies her to the bookstores, she leaves Mike in charge of Josh when they are with her on the signing tours.

The phone rings late in the night and she reaches to grab it before it wakes anyone else up.

"Sorry to call so late," her agent, Nancy, whispers as if her whispers will prevent anyone else from being disturbed by this call. "But I figured you'd want to know right away..." Nancy pauses for effect. "Oprah Winfrey wants you on her show in November to promote your book. She has made it one of her picks."

The author sits upright in her bed letting the covers fall, then collapses into her pillows. This is a dream come true.

"Are you there?" Nancy asks. "Are you okay?" But Nancy chuckles softly, she knows what is happening. The author is too overwhelmed to answer.

"Of course I'll do it," the author shouts forgetting the others sleeping in her house.

"Are you crazy?! Of course I'll do it." She repeats quietly as she can hear rustling from her boys' rooms.

"You gotta do something with that face before you go on national television," Josh says when she tells them the news in the morning. Mike looks like a raging bull ready to kill the bearer of such a message. Sean stares at her as if trying to see what it is that Josh is seeing. Sean is still young enough to love her just as she is and not be embarrassed by his aging mother.

When the boys have gone off to school, she turns all the lights on in the bathroom and looks at her face. Josh is right, no matter that his words stung her heart, he is right. How can she go on national television with this saggy old face of hers. She returns to the living room and starts to make phone calls. The Oprah show is in two months, she will have time to recover from the surgery and look good on television. The sales of her book have paid her bills and she has some cash to spend on herself. She is going to do it, she deserves it.

The initial appointment with the plastic surgeon lasts over an hour. He has his assistant take pictures of her from every angle to view every inch of her face, then calls her into his office to talk.

"Do you smoke," the surgeon asks.

"I quit six months ago," she answers with pride. *As soon as I sold my book*, she thinks to herself. It was a promise to herself as she wrote and rewrote the book.

"That's good," the surgeon continues. "That's exactly how long I require that my patients quit before I do surgery." And they begin discussing exactly what he will do to improve her looks. The surgeon suggests several procedures that she readily rejects. She doesn't really want to look twenty again or drastically different, just rested and refreshed.

"I'll check with the hospital to make sure they have a surgery suite available," he says. "But I have an opening in a week."

She nods in agreement and he calls his assistant to set up the time and date. The surgeon admonishes her regarding the recovery time and how she will have to rest for the best results.

"And," the surgeon warns, "No smoking for at least six months after the surgery." He gives her a stern look.

"I have no intention of starting again," she states. "Not for aesthetics, but so I can live for my children. They need me for a while longer." The surgeon smiles at her as she stands. She leaves his office with a light heart and smile on her face.

A week later, Cheryl drives her to the hospital. Cheryl has come to stay with her and take care of the boys while she is recuperating.

"You know he's going to keep dragging you back into court," Cheryl says when they arrive at the hospital. "He can't stand that you're a success without him." Their conversation for the ride to the hospital had focused on her ex-husband who is now suing for sole custody of the boys because of her new, "unstable" lifestyle.

"I know," she answers. "But I can't let him drag my life down any more. Besides, I have equal money to face off with him now and he can't back me down anymore."

"He's going to find a way to use this against you, you know?" Cheryl asks pulling her own cheeks up to indicate the facelift. "Are you sure you want to go through with it?" Cheryl is secretly pleased, and a little bit jealous that her long time friend is going to do something about her looks.

"I can't go on Oprah looking like this," she slumps in the passenger seat, her hands framing her face. She sought out the best of the plastic surgeons she could afford. It was humiliating to have the pictures taken in the bright lights and the surgeon point out every flaw that showed up. They had opted for procedures that would erase about ten years off her weary face and, she hoped, make her look more like the happy younger woman she was before her divorce.

Cheryl stays with her in the pre-op area and is in the room when she finally opens her eyes after surgery. Her face is heavily bandaged and talk is difficult, but Cheryl fills in the gaps.

"You wanna mirror, Mummy?" Cheryl asks with a grin. "It's hard to tell if there is a human being in there."

She reaches up to touch the bandages that will come off in a day or two. She feels like a mummy and would like to sleep a thousand years.

By the time she is to appear on the Oprah show, the bruises and swelling have all subsided. Even Cheryl has to admit that her friend looks great. Not strangely different, as Cheryl had feared, but rested and like her younger self. Cheryl quit her legal secretary job and is working for and living with her friend. After Oprah, they are going to Europe where the book is selling even better than in the United States. After the European book signing tour they are doing a US tour and Cheryl is now employed as her personal assistant and accompanying her on the trips.

"As long as that doesn't mean I'm your personal babysitter." Cheryl admonished her when she asked Cheryl to work for her.

She is thrilled with the surgery results, but that is not on her mind at the moment. She met with Oprah and her directors earlier in the week. They requested that she bring her boys with her to the show since the characters in her book are based on them. Yesterday her ex-husband served her with legal papers blocking her from allowing Mike and Josh to be shown on stage. She needs to decide if she will allow Sean to appear without his brothers. She doesn't want to emphasize the fact that they are half brothers to anyone. As far as she is concerned, they are brothers, from the same womb. She will discuss with Oprah and the producers how to proceed when they all arrive at the studio.

For now she is enjoying the limo ride through Chicago and the celebrity treatment she is receiving. The boys, and Josh's band members, are in another limo following hers, hoping for national coverage for their band. The other band members' parents having all signed waivers allowing them to be seen and perform on the Oprah show.

11

JOSHUA

The sun peaks through the unadorned windows, highlighting the dust motes floating in the air. A large black and white cat sprints around the corner to greet the young man opening the door.

"Hey, Kiva," Josh reaches down to scratch the cat behind the ears as she stretches up to rub her head on his hip. His long black hair falls to obscure his face and he absently pushes it behind his ears. "Did ya miss me?" He picks the cat up and cradles her in his arms. He kicks the door shut with a thud and walks into the house. "Mom," he says. "Mom" a decibel louder. "MOM!" He yells into the empty spaces. He waits impatiently for a response, looking down the long hallway to what used to be his room. "Where is she?" he asks the cat purring in his arms. He walks past the kitchen to the sliding glass doors leading to the back yard. He drops the cat on the floor as he opens the door. Two dogs race each other to reach him as he steps onto the shaded patio. He scans the fenced yard until his eyes light on the graying golden retriever painfully and slowly raising up from a hollow under the ironwood tree. The dog ambles slowly toward him, tail wagging. The other two dogs dance and bounce around Josh, but he only has eyes for the old golden making her way tacross the yard.

"Hey, Lucky," he says as he gently grabs the dog's jowls, squatting to look into the clouded brown eyes. "How are you old girl?" The dog nuzzles her head into his lap and whines. Absently scratching the almost white head, Josh looks anxiously around the yard. He half expects Mom to emerge from around a corner with her gardening gear on. He is prepared for the accusations that will fly between them, but she doesn't make an appearance.

When he spots Manuel's old straw hat over the fence in the horse pasture, he gently pushes Lucky away from him and heads for the gate to the barn. Lucky stays in the shade of the patio cover where there is a soft bed for her to lie on. The two other dogs accompany Josh to the gate. He slips out to the horse corrals leaving the dogs to push their noses through the wrought iron gate while watching him. Mom's old grey truck is parked beside the barn loaded with hay and grain that Manuel is moving into the storage area of the barn.

"*Hola*, Manuel," Josh says to the short brown man, "*Como estas*?"

"*Senor* Josh," says the dark skinned, wiry little man in the straw hat, with a sad smile. This is the son that causes *Senora* so much upset. Despite working for Josh's mom since she's owned this house and property, Manuel speaks little English and still pronounces the name more like "Yosh." Josh wishes his mom or Michael were here to speak Spanish with Manuel. He always meant to learn the language, but too many other things got in the way.

"*Senor* Josh," Manuel says again. "I find gate *abierto*," Manuel pauses, "ahh, open. *Caballito* es beeg mess. Maybe she running in desert again." Manuel hesitates, knowing that the young man is hard pressed to understand him. Manuel feels it is imperative to let him know what has happened since he has not seen *Senora* this morning. Josh leans toward the man, head cocked and listening attentively. Manuel's demeanor indicates concern and Josh is trying to catch every nuance of what the man is saying.

"Was the lock on the gate?" asks Josh after a moments pause to digest and decipher what Manuel has told him.

"No, *senor*," Manuel looks ashamed. "I not find the lock and gate is open."

Josh smiles, his mom's little Arab is quite adept at opening the most intricate of gate latches with her flexible lips and strong teeth. If someone forgot to put the lock on the gate it is no surprise that the horse escaped from her corral and even the fence surrounding the property. As if to demonstrate her ability, the little horse walks over to Josh and starts to "lip" his arm, tugging at his shirt as she gets the material in her teeth. When she tires of this game she stretches her lips and explores every inch of his skin and clothing until she reaches his long, dyed black hair. She pulls a clump of hair into her mouth with her pink tongue and starts to chew on it.

"Hey, Jamila," Josh smiles and pushes the horse away. "Stop that." The mare pushes back at him with her nose. She then spins with a meaningless buck and walks back to the pile of hay to eat. Josh finger combs the spit and hay residue that Jamila's taste testing has left in his hair.

"One saddle gone, too," says Manuel. Concern is

written all over his face.

"Is it the old two tone brown one with no conchos?" Josh asks after a long pause.

Manuel thinks for a moment then nods.

"Mom's been talking about taking it in to be repaired since before I moved out," Josh says, "I guess she finally got around to it." The little brown man looks partially relieved. Still a look of concern that knows no language barrier passes between them.

Josh returns to the house, letting the shade of indoors give relief to his eyes from the harsh desert sun. All three dogs follow him into the house, but only Lucky follows him to his room at the end of the long hall. The dog plops into her bed in the corner of the room with a huff. Josh falls onto his own bed to stare at the ceiling. It is a ceiling that he and Mom painted deep, velvet blue. Embedded in the ceiling are small twinkling lights that mimic the constellations. He and Mom had done this together when she had the house built. He still loves to lie on his bed and look at the "stars" despite being a mature nineteen year old now.

"Mom," he calls out, "Mom!" he calls louder, "MOM," he yells. **"MOM,"** he shrieks and waits for the response. The only answer is Lucky's snoring from the corner of his room.

12

MORGUE

"Left breast has a surgical scar on it." Ralph Emerson lowers the sheet to expose the small, flattened breasts of the cadaver. "It is a very neat scar, so I would assume that it is the result of a surgical incision, rather than the repair of a wound of some sort." His gloved hand points to a small white line on her left breast. But Roger Albright is too engrossed in his notebook and writing to see where he is pointing.

13

FALL 1978

The paper crinkles under her naked butt as she shifts her weight on the exam table. She clutches the hospital gown up around her breasts as if to protect them from the words the doctor might say.

"Everything looks great, except for the lump in your left breast." The doctor is barely older than her, but has the air of authority that her white coat affords her. "I'd like to schedule you for an excision and biopsy as soon as possible. It is most likely nothing..."

Doctor Volbe's words drone in her head like a pesky mosquito, but she is no longer paying any attention. *What if it's not benign?* she thinks. Hell, despite the women's movement, everyone knows that a woman in the States is defined by her breasts. She is only twenty-three years old, isn't even married yet, hasn't had any children, and she wants to nurse them when she has them...

"Get dressed," the doctor's voice interrupts her thoughts, "and we'll discuss your options. I'd like to schedule the excision as soon as possible. With your permission, I'll reserve surgery as soon as I can."

She nods and slides forward on the paper covered table, the paper sticking to her butt and pulling off the table. She gets dressed in a fog of thought and walks the twenty steps to Dr. Volbe's office. It seems to take her hours to get there. She sits stiffly on the edge of the chair.

"Have you ever had a mammogram?" The doctor asks from across her paper strewn desk.

"No." Her eyes are wide with fear.

"Doesn't matter." Dr. Volbe tries to look reassuring. "I'm sending you down for one right now."

"Okay." Her eyes are wide and distant.

Dr. Volbe comes over and puts a cold hand on her shoulder, "Don't worry," she says. "I'm sure that it's nothing to be worried about."

The young woman walks out to the front desk in a fog of conflicting thoughts.

"They're waiting for you in radiology, right now." The receptionist hands the young woman a prescription page.

"Just give them this and they'll get you right in." Her eyes hold a look of empathy. "I told them it was an emergency."

Dr. Volbe walks into the reception area, "Come right back up here when you're done down there, and I should have you scheduled for an appointment with Doctor Carroll. He's one of the best breast men around here." The doctor looks the young woman directly in the eyes. "You'll be fine."

The prescription reads "Emergency Mammogram" therefore she only has to wait for two hours before she is seen. The x-rays are painful and embarrassing but she is on her way back to Dr. Volbe's office immediately afterwards.

"Well," says Dr. Volbe, holding up the x-ray so that they both can see it, "it's well defined and appears contained." She looks at her patient, "I would guess that it is a fibroid adenoma, but I made an appointment for you to see Dr. Carroll this afternoon." She looks at her watch, "in fact your appointment is in twenty minutes."

Dr. Carroll is in the same complex and does not leave his new patient waiting. Naked for the third time that day, she clutches the gown around her breasts and listens as this doctor reiterates the news.

"I certainly agree with Dr. Volbe," he says looking carefully at the x-ray against the brightness of the viewing lights in his office. "It appears to be a fibroid adenoma, but we'll get it out of there and biopsy it tomorrow." He reads the fear in his new patient's eyes and adds, "Don't worry, we'll be fine."

Why the hell do they always have to say "we," she thinks, *it's MY body you're cutting into.* But she listens to the pre-op instructions carefully. She'll have to get Cheryl to drive her to the hospital and home again afterward.

"The biggest question is..." Dr Carroll pauses to be sure that he has her full attention, "if you need a mastectomy do you want me to do it while you are still under anesthesia or do you want to wake up and decide then?" He starts to say something further when she

62

interrupts him.

"I insist on knowing the results of the biopsy first and making the decision then," she says firmly. "No mastectomy until I make that decision with the information I need."

Dr. Carroll smiles, she is a surprise to him. She looks scared but is in control of her emotions enough to think for herself. Most of his patients are too scared to be quite this adamant. He nods to let her know that he accepts her decision.

The next morning she waits with her friend Cheryl. Cheryl strokes her sweaty, shaking hands, and talks incessantly about nonsense until the orderly takes her into surgery.

A very handsome face tells her that he is going to put her to sleep. She laughs quietly; in her line of work as a veterinary assistant that term is a euphemism that means euthanasia. The next thing she remembers is Dr. Carroll and Dr. Volbe standing over her.

"It was benign......"

"..no damage to milk ducts......"

"Only a small incision..."

And their voices drone on while the young woman closes her eyes and seeks to regain that lovely plateau she had been visiting with the help of the anesthesia.

14

JOSHUA

Josh continues to stare uneasily at the ceiling in his room, while Lucky snores in the corner. *It's eerily quiet in here*, he thinks with a shiver, *Mom usually has music playing and is typing away at her computer. Even when she's out, the phone rings constantly.* As if in response to his thoughts the phone jars him out of his reverie. He runs to the office to check the caller ID, then hits the speaker button.

"I figured you'd be there when you weren't in the dorm." Mike's voice fills the room.

"Hello, Michael," Josh says. "Nice to hear from you, too." He rolls his eyes, knowing the grilling about to commence. Mike asks him about school, and his band, and Lindsay, his girlfriend, if he's gotten any new piercings. Josh avoids answering any of the questions directly as he doesn't think that Mike has any right to know. When Mike falls silent for a moment without the usual admonishments about Josh's attitude, Josh is disappointed. He realizes suddenly that Mike has actually tracked him down to their mother's house and not on his cell phone as he usually does. Josh begins to take in his surroundings. He is in his mom's office, usually forbidden territory. But something is very different. The desk is clean. The computer put away, no papers lying about, and no books pulled off the shelves. Josh considers mentioning these observations to Mike when Mike's voice interrupts his thoughts.

"Look, Josh," says Mike. "I talked to Sean earlier and he seemed worried about Mom."

"She's not here," says Josh suddenly forgetting exactly what he was going to say to Mike.

"I know," the speaker emits. "Do you know where she is?"

"I only know that she's on spring break like the rest of the school." Josh allows annoyance to grip his voice. "She didn't tell me about any plans to go anywhere. She only tells you, the responsible one, those kinds'a things." There is silence for a moment, then, with false brightness in his voice, "Hey, maybe she got a boyfriend and ran away to Mexico or sumthin. That would be cool."

"Aren't you supposed to be with Dad this week? While he's out there visiting?" asks Mike ignoring Josh's sarcasm.

"Yeah, well," Josh hesitates, he expects Mike to respond with his normal advice about how to act and talk, but Mike is not acting like his big brother today so he tries to goad him again. "I don't exactly like being around his latest girlfriend. You might like her though; she's about your age."

"Let it go," groans the speaker.

"They get younger every year," Josh says still trying for the desired reaction. "Pretty soon he'll be after Lindsay."

The speaker emits a long, deep sigh from the caller and then Josh can hear his brother talking to someone else with only a minimal effort to mask the fact.

"I gotta go," Mike says into the phone again, "I got a class in ten. I'm gonna try to get a flight out early so I can spend some time with Dad. Call me tomorrow, okay?"

"Sure," says Josh without conviction and hits the "end" button on the phone console. He is feeling a little lost because he did everything he knew to agitate his brother, but Mike was too focused on their mom's absence to react. He shrugs his shoulders and shakes his long hair out of his face.

Josh opens the second drawer down on the right hand side of the desk. Rummaging to the bottom of the drawer, he finds what he is seeking. A small white envelope with his name on the front. *Thank you, Mom*, he thinks as he tears open the envelope and pulls out several twenties. Despite the pain of having a best-selling author for a mom, not to mention that she is the writer in residence at his college, she always seems to remember his needs. He stuffs the bills into his wallet and heads out of the house. On his way, Josh walks through the garage. His mom's Hummer dominates the area and he briefly thinks about taking it and leaving his car. Lindsay loves to be seen around Tempe in the big vehicle and Mom bought it just to please him and his brothers. She rarely drives it. With a shrug he squeezes between the Hummer and the hybrid car that Mom drives most of the time. He'll take his Baja and save the gas money this time. But as he starts his vehicle he realizes that something is nagging him. It's not just Mike's refusal to rise to his taunts, but something else besides. He shrugs again, gets in his car, and roars down the drive to the gate, music blaring loudly, the dust obliterating the view behind him.

15

MORGUE

"Inside of left arm, running from wrist to crook of the elbow is a very faint, but wide scar. Looks like an injury that was not surgically attended to." Ralph Emerson is holding the cadaver's left hand tracing the visible scar with his forefinger. Roger Albright watches in fascination, overcoming for a moment his personal revulsion to the body on the table..

16

SPRING 1981

She bends over the schedule book, slumps her shoulders, and sighs. *We are booked, booked solid,* she thinks. Three cats to spay for Mrs. Doogan, one dental cleaning on a big dog, one dog for tumor removal, and appointments scheduled through the morning, right up to scheduled surgery time. Dr. Davis can move through appointments quickly, but it is Parvo season, and there are bound to be several sick dogs hospitalized today. They will join the rest of the vomiting and bloody diarrhea crew in the isolation ward. Silently, she curses the newly "discovered" disease that seems to hit the area in waves during the spring and fall.

"Oh well," she says aloud. "Time to clean up the puke and shit before they do it all over again." The receptionist, Donna, snorts in response, then resumes talking to the person on the phone. She heads down the hallway to prepare the hospital for more incoming patients.

"Technician to the front for a surgery drop off,"

69

the intercom blares, but it is barely audible over the noise of all the dogs in the hospital. Mrs. Doogan is dropping off three more of the feral cats that hunt her barn for her, to be spayed or neutered. The technician has prepared three cages right at chest level for them. Some of the cats are pretty wild and the technicians need them to be in cages at a level they can reach in to deposit or withdraw the cats quickly and safely.

She lugs two of the heavy "Have-A-Heart" traps, each with a cat in it, to the back of the hospital. The waiting rooms are crowded with people and pets and the phones can be heard ringing constantly. She grabs a heavy towel and gently and carefully tucks it around the cat in the cage. She lifts the scared cat in the towel up to the cage in front of her, deposits the cat, and slams the door to the cage before the cat can try to escape. *One down and two to go*, she sighs with relief as she puts the towel in position to grab the second cat. The cats are both in their cages, pushing against the stainless steel back of the cage. They both hiss angrily at her when she goes to the waiting room to grab the third trap from Mrs. Doogan. Just as she snags the last wild cat from its trap, and is lifting it to deposit it in the open cage, Donna rushes in with a yapping Pomeranian in her hands. Donna shoves the dog in the open cage, slams the cage door shut, and turns to leave.

"Hey Donna," she says. "I need that cage for this cat." Her hands are full of a struggling, hissing, writhing, snarling cat, only partially wrapped in the heavy towel.

Donna spins around with a huff and comes back to the bank of cages. She stands on tiptoe and opens the cage directly above the Pomeranian.

"Use this one," Donna says and runs off to answer the forever ringing phones.

With the screaming, writhing cat in her hands, she has no choice, and reaches up to aim the cat into the cage that Donna opened. She has to reach right past the Pomeranian's cage. The dog chooses this moment to restart its yapping, and adds lunging at the front of the cage to the action. The cat in her hands struggles and twists with intense fear, claws exposed. When the cat sees the cave-like sanctuary of the open cage above, it seeks purchase to jump in and hide. Its back claws find their grip on the inside of the technician's forearm and the cat pushes with all of its frightened strength.

She slams the cage door shut and examines the wound running from the tender inside of her wrist all the way to the crook of her elbow. It isn't bleeding much but is pretty wide. As she goes to the sink to wash the wound, the intercom demands a technician up front again. A cursory rinse and she is off and running again.

When she wakes up the next morning, her arm feels like a fully expanded blood pressure cuff is on it. She looks at the arm and her eyes fly open. She bolts upright and sucks in her breath, her head swimming alarmingly. The arm looks like a stuffed sausage with a road map drawn on it. She is sweating heavily. Her dogs are whining to be let out and fed, so she cradles her swollen arm and swings her feet toward the floor. Her head spins with the motion, but she has to get up and feed her critters. She stands slowly, holding the side rail of her waterbed for balance.

As she stumbles around the house, bumping into walls, and tripping over carpet threads, she realizes that she needs a doctor. Somehow she makes it to the phone to call her neighbor to take her to the hospital.

"Cat Scratch Fever," says the young intern in the emergency room after he has looked at the grotesquely swollen arm, heard the story of the inury, and taken her temperature. She starts to laugh at him when she notices that his face is deadly serious.

"No, not the song," he continues with a sneer. "But a real conglomeration of bacteria caused, quite often, by a cat scratch, and quite serious if not treated properly. Cat's harbor a lot of nasty bacteria under their nails."

She gulps back the laughter that threatens to escape her throat, as Ted Nugent's tune spins through her brain. The treatment is simple, rest, fluids, and antibiotics. She'll be fine, but the arm will bear a scar forever.

17

MIKE

Mike pulls his head further into his warm parka to block the cold wind. He reminds himself of the turtles he used to catch when he was a small boy. *As soon as Physics is done, I'm going home to warm up*, he thinks. He reaches into a pocket and pulls out his cell phone. Pushing a few buttons with his gloved hand, while he walks to his next class, he finds relief from the wind in a building entryway. He listens with a frown as the phone rings and rings in Arizona. Finally, the answering machine picks up. Mike has to smile when he hears her new message. "I'm probably out doing research for my next book. At least that's my latest excuse for riding all day..."

It is almost exactly what he had said to her at Christmas when he'd heard the message she had then. The old message said, "I'm sorry that I'm not available right now, I am doing research for my latest book. Please leave a message at the sound of the tone."

"Who are you trying to kid?" Michael told her at Christmas, before Josh exploded and ruined everyone's holiday. "Everyone knows you're not out doing research, you're out riding in the desert on your crazy mare."

Mom laughed at the time, and the Christmas festivities went on, but apparently she hadn't forgotten the comment.

"Hey Mom," he says after the beep. "I'm trying to get a flight home right after class tomorrow instead of coming next week. I'll let you know if it works out, okay? Call me on my cell phone when you get this message."

He ends the call and speed dials his father's cell phone number.

"Hey Dad," he says. "How's the Arizona weather?"

He listens for a moment, and then says. "Look, I really can't talk right now. I have a class in a few minutes. I just wanted to let you know that I'm working on getting a flight out of here tomorrow instead of next week."

After a pause he says, "Thanks, I really appreciate the offer, but I already called Mom and asked her to pick me up at the airport, so that shouldn't be a problem."

He listens to the phone, rolls his eyes and sighs away from the phone, "Don't worry, I'll call Josh to pick me up if I don't hear from Mom, okay? Not a problem."

"No," he says, again rolling his eyes but keeping his voice level. "I'll stay at Mom's house. I still have my own room and all my stuff there."

"I know," he adds after a pause, "I love you too." He ends the call and turns to enter the building for refuge from the cold wind. He shakes the snow off his parka and climbs the stairs two at a time to make it to his class on time.

18

MORGUE

Ralph gently holds the body's right hand and turns it so that the inside of the wrist is facing him. "Strange scar on the inside of the right wrist. Looks like an old burn. The scar is curved... like it was burned on a very hot curved object...

19

SEPTEMBER 1991

"Don't forget that I'm going to Fire Island this weekend," Michael says as he enters the kitchen and grabs her plate out of her hand. He wolfs down the pancake on it and smiles maliciously at her, challenging her to say something. She just sighs and pours more batter into the hot pan to make herself another pancake. Their two boys are happily eating pancakes, in awe that their father is home, and sitting down to a meal with them.

"They don't have a phone out there so you won't be able to reach me all weekend." He looks at her pointedly. "If you have an emergency, you can page me and I'll find a phone to call you back."

She merely stares at him before turning back to check her pancake. *Yeah, your precious pager,* she thinks, *you live your life by that thing.*

A few nights ago his pager went off during foreplay. Michael stopped to check and see who was calling.

"Hold that thought," he said, "it's Ellen and I have to call her right away." Then he left the bed to make a call. He has to put even sex on hold since his longtime love is calling again. Stop ANYTHING to talk to Ellen.

Shit, she thinks, *we even moved to this town just so he could be closer to her.* She sniggers at the memory of Ellen then moving to North Carolina soon after they moved here.

She flips her pancake and is about to put it on her plate when Michael walks up to the stove, puts his fork into the pancake, his hand pressing on hers to keep her from moving. She feels the intense heat where her wrist is searing to the edge of the old iron frying pan, but she won't move or cringe, she just stares back into his eyes.

"MMMM, these are good pancakes, aren't they, boys?" he says aloud, turns his back to the boys, and growls quietly into her ear, "Don't you even say a word to the boys. You've done enough damage to 'em, this is just between you and me." He snags the pancake, flops it on his plate, then spins. His back to her, he sits at the table with the boys. He tells them about his trip to Fire Island and all the fun he will have on the beach.

She runs cold water over the tender inside of her wrist and notes the bright red line already forming blisters. Her stomach growls and she pours more batter into the hot pan, thinking about the divorce papers he'd served her with yesterday. He's been planning this trip to Fire Island with "some friends" for a couple of weeks, saying she wouldn't know any of the friends he was going with. She never questioned him although they have been married for ten years now and she doubts that he has many friends she hasn't met. His pager has gone off repeatedly, late at night, since he informed her of the trip, and he's made many late night return calls. He says that he needs this trip to think about their marriage and figure out what he needs to do.

I guess he's figured out what to do, she thinks.

She sends Mikey off to school, and gets Joshua to take a nap so she has a few free minutes. She is cleaning up the breakfast dishes when the phone rings. A strange woman asks her if she is Michael's wife.

I guess I still am, she thinks as she answers positively. The woman is from the airlines confirming Michael's flight to Charlotte, N.C. Her heart drops into the pit of her stomach. The strangeness of the last few weeks suddenly settles on her like a pall. Michael's mysterious trip to Fire Island with "friends" he claims she won't know, Ellen calling at all hours, and him rushing to talk to her in private. Ellen is, the only person they know who lives in North Carolina. She realizes that he isn't going to Fire Island with some mysterious friends; he is going to see Ellen again. This time he's filed for divorce first so obviously he has some really special plans.

She sits staring into space for a moment, still holding the phone in hand, letting the realization sink into her conscious mind. She shakes her head to try to force the jumble of her thoughts into some semblance of order. Then she calls her friend, David. He is the only friend who has stuck by her since Michael started spreading the stories of them having an affair. Of course, she and David know the truth; others are just listening to lies and innuendo. Michael had, in fact, accused her of having an affair with David as a reason for suing her for divorce. Who else can she contact? She feels so alone and hurt. David is his usual calm self when he answers the phone. He listens quietly as she cries out her woes. He has heard so many stories of Michael's atrocities that this is no surprise to him.

"Well, he's gone this weekend," David finally says. "So you have the kids. Why don't we get together next weekend and talk? Can you do that?"

They finalize plans to go to the Renaissance Fair and spend the day together. Doing something distracting, yet with time to allow them to talk. She hangs up feeling a little less alone. Since they met, she and David have talked for hours and hours. It is so nice for her to have someone actually listen to her for a change.

Michael leaves on Friday, as planned, and she has not confronted him with her knowledge. She calls Ellen's house on Saturday with an emergency question for Michael. Ellen tries to claim that he is not there and even threatens her with harassment charges after the the third call. After the fourth call, Ellen relents and gets Michael out of the shower to talk to his soon to be ex-wife. Michael comes home from North Carolina on Sunday instead of the planned Tuesday return. He is in a rage from the moment he gets home, but she doesn't care. She knows that his anger is at being caught in another lie.

The burn on her wrist is scabbing over and she hopes that it will be mostly healed by the time she sees David. She doesn't want David to see the physical injury that Michael has inflicted, she just wants to spill her woes to a friendly ear.

But they don't talk. When she meets David at his apartment, she bursts into tears. The false bravado she's worn for weeks finally falls apart when she sees a friendly face. He puts his arms around her and holds her until the tears slow enough for her to talk. She tells him about Michael's latest activities, even showing him her burned wrist. He holds her close and lets her wail, murmuring about nothing into her hair. As her crying continues he

80

begins to kiss the top of her head and rub her back gently. When the crying finally stops, she looks up at his warm brown eyes and they kiss. The kiss is friendly at first and then becomes more fervent. She reaches her arms up around his neck and, finally, they do what Michael has been accusing them of for months; they make love. Not once, but ttwice, and she lays next to him feeling warm and safe until an intruding thought makes her jump out of the bed. They haven't used birth control.

20

MORGUE

Doctor Emerson, still holding the body's right hand, traces a jagged white line on the palm.

"Deep, poorly repaired scar on the palm of the right hand. Starts between the forefinger and second finger and extends to life line. I can see the marks from sutures having been placed, the scar is jagged and uneven, not like a surgical incision. And the scar appears to be old..."

21

FALL 1962

Her father holds the bike upright and it looks like a black race horse to her, ready to be mounted, and take off running. The girl puts her hands to her mouth and screams silently. Her father stands to the side of the bike, beaming at his daughter's response.

"It's the latest thing in racing bikes." He looks at her with solemn pride. "It has three speeds. You can shift them over here." He points to a lever by the left hand grip. "And these are your brakes." Her dad continues. "You have to learn to pull up on them to stop the bike." He demonstrates the brakes. "If you try to stop by using the pedals, all you'll do is pedal backwards." He smiles at his precocious seven year old. "I want you to ride here in front of the house where I can see you for a while, okay?"

The girl doesn't answer, but absently nods her head. Her eyes are absorbed in the gleaming black paint, the chrome handle bars, and all the wires running from the handlebars to the brakes and the thing her father calls the derailer. It is the first bike she has ever seen without fenders, but it doesn't need fenders. It is a beautiful thoroughbred in her eyes.

"Beauty," she says quietly. "Black Beauty"

"Just ride it carefully," says her mother with a look of concern. Mom can remember the many trips to the emergency room with this child. More than the rest of her children put together. She doesn't approve of the gift, but her husband has never listened to anything she's said before, she can't expect him to now.

The girl grabs the hand-grips, kicks up the stand and swings her leg over to mount the bike. It is a thoroughbred, tall with skinny tires, just like the skinny legs of the horse. She tests out the brakes and listens while her father tells her how to shift the gears. Her impatience shows in the rocking back and forth of the bike. She is in the starting gate waiting for it to open. When Dad tells her to ride, she is off in a flash.

She and her friend, Jimmy take off toward the sheep pasture at the end of the road. The new black bike wobbles and veers as the girl seeks to control it. Her mother turns away, and enters the house, shaking her head, and wringing her hands. Her father sits in the shade of the front porch to watch and shout instructions.

For Christmas that same year she gets a pull bell for her bike to warn others that she is coming. Santa knows just what she needs. Dad helps her mount it on "Black Beauty's" handlebar directly in front of the right hand-grip. She has only to reach forward with a right finger to pull the lever and send the warning. By early the next spring she is an expert at handling her new bike. It is still a little big for her, but the neighborhood races belong to her once again. She is ecstatic. She thought those days were over when her old bike was stolen. Now she knows that the old bike was a plow horse next to this new thoroughbred of hers.

"On your mark... Get set..." Jimmy looks around at the other kids in the race. It is his brother, some friends, and her. She always wins. He waits until she seems to be daydreaming, "GO" he shouts and looks back. She has been daydreaming and is now behind everyone else, pedaling hard to make up the difference.

It doesn't take her long to catch and pass everyone. She has the newest and fastest bike in the neighborhood and no one can beat her. If Jimmy were being honest he would admit that she has always been the fastest, even with her old, rusted, one speed bike, but he is too competitive when it comes to their bike races.

She pulls up hard on her brakes and stops at the sheep pasture fence, a grin splitting her freckled face. Jimmy is only a bike length behind. The rest of the kids surround them and congratulate her. She is tops in the neighborhood, again. Secretly, all of the kids were relieved when her old bike was stolen as they thought that they would have a chance at winning one of the many races they hold each week.

"I gotta go home and do some homework," says Tommy as he turns and rides away on his bike. Soon all of the kids are leaving except her and Jimmy.

"Let's go ride Joe's hill," says Jimmy. In an otherwise pretty flat area, Joe's hill is the highest point around. It takes some effort to reach the top of the hill, but the thrill of the speeds reached going down are worth the effort.

"Let's go," she agrees readily and both children set off toward the road in front of Joe's house.

Both riders are huffing and puffing by the time they reach the top of the hill. Without a word of discussion, they stop to rest at the top and catch their breath.

"Betcha can't make it down the hill no handed," Jimmy challenges her.

"Watch me," she replies.

She starts off pedaling easily then lets the slope take charge of her speed. With caution released to the breeze flowing through her hair, she lets go of both hand grips. She closes her eyes briefly just to feel the complete freedom of flying, but even she is too scared to ride this way for long. The road at the bottom of the hill curves around a saguaro and she leans to steer the bike without gripping the handlebars. As she approaches the end of the pavement, she grabs the grips and pulls hard on the brakes, sliding sideways off the paved road onto the dirt crossroad. She looks back up the hill to see Jimmy still sitting there watching her.

"C'mon," she calls to him. "You can do it."

"Come back up and we'll go down together," he replies.

So she rides back up the hill, standing on the pedals to fight gravity, and reach the top. She is puffing hard from the effort and can hear her heart beating in her ears.

"Let's go," yells Jimmy as soon as she reaches the top. He starts pedaling down the hill.

Still winded, she pushes off the top of the hill, pedaling hard to catch up to him. Jimmy lets go of his hand grips as soon as she is next to him. She steadies her bike and, with Jimmy on her right, she too lets go of the grips. They coast down the hill side by side, hands in the air until they come to the curve.

Jimmy's bike starts to wobble and he grips the handlebars to steer it. When she sees his bike wobbling, she leans further to the left to steer her bike away from his. But she leans too hard and the bike starts to fall. In a panic, she reaches for the hand-grips, but her balance is already off, and the sudden motion to grab the hand grips causes her bike to turn sideways, and slide into the fence post past the saguaro. Desperately she clings to the grips as the bike grinds to a sudden halt. She continues forward, shot past the fence post by her forward motion. She feels a sharp pain in the palm of her right hand and hears the bell ring its warning before she hits the ground with a dull thud.

She stands up and shakes herself, then looks at her beloved "Black Beauty." The bike is a mess; the fork is bent, the front tire flat and the rim dented, the handlebars are sideways. But it is the bell that catches her eye. The lever is broken off and there is something hanging from the sharp remainder of the lever.

The pain in her right hand makes her look away from the bike and at herself. Suddenly she bursts into tears. She now knows that what is hanging from the bell on her bike is the long tendril of skin missing from her right palm. Starting between her forefinger and second finger is a gaping, bleeding tear.

"Are you alright?" Jimmy asks as he runs over to her. His freckled face blanches when he sees her hand. "Get home," he says as he gently pushes her in that direction. "I'll bring Black Beauty home." He puts his arm around her waist and guides her towards her house. "I promise I'll bring the bike home."

With that assurance, she runs home, wailing loudly, and holding her right hand to her chest.

Her mother runs out of the house, wiping her hands on the apron tied to her waist, to see what all the noise is about. When she sees the blood on the girl's chest, she grabs her daughter, and pulls her into her lap, to examine the damage. Relief floods Mom's face when she realizes that the blood is from the hand and not the little girl's chest. Mom sends her older sister to get the neighbor to drive them to the hospital. Soon Frank is pulling into the driveway in his old blue station wagon.

"It won't be pretty," the grey haired doctor in the emergency room tells them. "She lost a wide piece of skin and the cut is deep. It will take subcutaneous sutures as well as skin sutures to close the wound and it could limit the use of her forefinger." The doctor looks at the little girl sitting in the big man's lap. "It'll mean that you won't be able to ride your bike until after the stitches come out." The little girl allows a few tears to fall with this statement.

"She won't be able to swim as long as the stitches are in. I'll put a wrap on her hand to keep those fingers together and allow the area to heal."

Her mom listens intently to the doctor's instructions. Frank cuddles the girl closely. He is smiling. She is curled in his lap, despite her height, her long legs folded up to her chest, her bandaged hand held out in the front like a surrender flag. He knows that this is not his last trip to the emergency room with this child.

The girl spends the weeks with her hand bandaged figuring out how to fix Black Beauty. Jimmy helps her and, when she needs tools, or strength, she asks Frank.

22

CONSUELO

Consuelo punches her code into the key pad and opens the heavy, carved wooden door. The silence of the house surprises her even though Manuel told her that he had not seen *Senora* all day yesterday.

The morning sun slants into the house from the eastern windows and the three dogs approach Consuelo, yawning, and stretching as she closes the door. The woman absently scratches each of their heads in turn, and pushes past them, on her way to the pantry to get them food.

"*Hola*, sleepyheads," Consuelo remarks to the canine audience. "*Hombre*?" As if it can understand Spanish, one of the dogs begins to spin, jump, and bark excitedly. Lucky, the old Golden Retriever, stiffly backs away from the action and wags her tail. The third dog walks on its hind legs as if trying to look into Consuelo's eyes.

"*Donde es tu mama*?" Consuelo asks as she sets

the food dishes down for the dogs and glances around the house. The dogs eat merrily in reply. On rare occasions *Senora* has slept late and not greeted Consuelo when she came in. Usually she is in the kitchen drinking orange juice, having fed the dogs and cats. *Senora* works from home most of the time, so she usually greets Consuelo with instructions before she goes into the office down the hall. The kitchen has an abandoned feel to Consuelo as she looks around.

Three cats are soon circling Consuelo's legs and meowing, so she gets some food for them too. She has to feed them in the laundry room on a counter so that the dogs won't eat their food. Pressing issues under control, Consuelo now has time to notice the house itself. It gleams in its cleanliness. There is not even a stitch of clothing waiting to be washed. Consuelo is cook, housekeeper, and friend to *Senora*, and this is the day she is scheduled to clean the house. Consuelo has worked here long enough that *Senora* has gotten past the need to clean the house prior to Consuelo's scheduled cleaning. But the house is spotless, except for a glass with dried milk in it in the sink, and a nearly empty bag of Cheetos on the counter. Consuelo knows that Sean is staying with that man he calls "Dad" so she doesn't expect to have as much cleaning to do. Sean does tend to mess things up like most teenagers. But the house looks as if it is ready for a tour to come through.

Tiptoeing through the laundry room, Consuelo notes the clean, folded laundry and gleaming floor tiles. The workout room is the same, and Consuelo peeks into Senora's bedroom with a heart beating so guiltily fast that she feels it might jump out of her chest. She prays that she won't disturb *Senora*.

"*Senora*," she whispers. But she can see the bed and the only evidence that anything has slept there are three circular indentations in the comforter; perfect size and shape for three sleeping cats. Muse, the big tabby cat is standing guard at the window watching Consuelo. The cat growls and hisses when Consuelo walks into the room.

"*Senora,*" she says loudly. "*Donde estas*?"

Muse growls in response.

Consuelo sidesteps to the bathroom, not taking her eyes off the angry cat she just fed, and checks the tub and shower. Both are empty and glistening in their cleanliness. She quickly leaves the room and checks the rest of the house. She enters the office with some trepidation. This is *Senora's* private space. Consuelo has never even cleaned in here, but she needs to see if there is some clue as to where Senora might be. The office is spotless. The only thing on the usually paper strewn desk is the phone somehow left off it's charging cradle. Consuelo grabs the phone and, after a quick glance around, leaves the office. She can't explain her panic, but she knows that something is wrong. Maybe it's the clean house, maybe the animals not being fed... She isn't sure. She only knows that her boss and friend hasn't been home, hasn't left a note or called to say where she was going, and that is wrong. She presses the speed dial for Josh's cell phone, he is the closest and more grown up than Sean, who is with "that man." She opens the arcadia door to the patio. She needs to find Manuel to have him help her right now. While she waits for Josh to answer his phone, she motions Manuel into the house. He has been married to Consuelo a long time and she is not one to panic, so Manuel searches the house from one expanse to the other. He finds no evidence that anyone other than Sean and Josh have been there.

23

MORGUE

"Probably the most significant scar is this one." The medical examiner pulls the sheet down to the body's pubic area and points to the low abdomen, tracing a faint scar with his gloved hand.

"Midline incision, low abdomen, runs through the pubic hair."

Albright is looking at the medical examiner with rapt attention.

"It's a Cesarean Section scar if I ever saw one." Emerson looks pointedly at Roger and notes that he has the young man's full attention now. "It's not a recent scar, but significant. On palpation, I can feel the scar on the uterus, too." He is looking at the body's face, his head tilted to the side, a frown creasing his forehead.

"This woman is someone's mom..."

24

DECEMBER 17, 1984

She tosses the blanket off despite the cold permeating the room, and rolls her rounded belly onto her other side. It proves to be too cold with no covers, so she pulls the blanket back up over her belly. Michael bursts out in a growl of snoring just as she is about to fall back to sleep, so she kicks him in his naked butt. Michael sputters but doesn't wake up.

"Damn you," she whispers into the dark room. "It's not fair that you can sleep."

Suddenly her stomach muscles contract in a dull pressure and she groans. As she starts to roll off the bed, she feels hot liquid leaking between her legs and feels another cramp in her abdomen. The liquid is pouring out of her now, wetting the bed thoroughly. When the cramp stops, she rolls over and shakes Michael's shoulder.

"Mike," she says and shakes him again. "Mike," she says louder

"Uh," he grunts in reply. "Sup?" And the snoring resumes.

"Wake up, Mike," she says loudly and shakes his shoulders roughly. "Wake up. I think my water broke."

"Mmm," he groans. "Too early."

"Mike!" She has maneuvered her bloated body out of bed and is leaning over, supporting herself on the edge of the bed, as another contraction punches her in the abdomen.

"Mike, get up," she says loudly. "This baby is coming today. My water broke."

Michael rolls over on the bed and swipes his hand across her side feeling the moisture in the sheets.

"No," he mumbles, "you just wet the bed." He rolls over to the edge of the bed farthest from her and resumes snoring.

She stands up slowly and is walking around the end of the bed, when the snoring quite suddenly breaks off, and Michael sits up in bed.

"Your water broke" he says loudly. "What are you doin' standin' on the rug? You'll ruin it." He quickly rolls out of bed and jogs toward her.

"C'mon," he says, putting his arm around her extended waist. "I'll help you get to the bathroom."

"Don't bother," she pushes him out of her way and stomps into the bathroom. At the birthing classes they attended, the nurse said to take a shower if you can't sleep and the contractions are not regular yet. She turns on the water in the shower hot and fast.

She is just about to step into the steaming shower when Michael peers around the doorway, his watch in his hand

.

"Tell me when you get a contraction," he says plopping down on the closed toilet seat and scrubbing his face with his free hand.

"Why did you have to do this at four o'clock in the morning?" he shouts over the roar of the shower. "Couldn't you wait until later?"

He drops his head against the back of the toilet and she can hear him snoring again as another contraction hits her. When the cramp releases her, she peeks around the shower curtain and, seeing that Michael is sleeping again, she grabs his watch and notes the time. Three minutes later she is grabbed by another contraction that leaves her hanging onto the shower head to keep from falling. When the pain passes, she reaches out of the shower for Michael's watch, and checks the time. She turns the water off and grabs her towel from the back of the toilet. Michael's head thunks harshly on the toilet tank as he had been using the towel as a pillow while he slept.

"Look," he says, rubbing the back of his head, "they told us the first baby is always slow to come, so there's no rush." He walks out of the bathroom and back to the bedroom, yawning, and stretching

.

She throws open the shower curtain and says, "My contractions are three minutes apart and regular. You tell this baby its going to take a long time to come."

"I'll call the midwife," he says from the bedroom. She can hear him opening dresser drawers and picking up the phone as she dries off. Another contraction grips her in its power, sending her falling to her knees in front of the toilet. She briefly thinks that it has been years since she prayed to the porcelain god, but the strength of the contraction cuts off the chuckle she'd wanted. When the pain stops, she grabs Michael's watch again. Two minutes forty-eight seconds.

Damn, she thinks, *they're getting even closer.* Her hands shake and her breath comes in puffs as if she has just run a hard race. *I'm not ready for this*, she thinks as she gets dressed in comfortable clothes. *Who am I kidding thinking I can be anyone's mom?* Before she can worry herself any further, Michael enters the bathroom with the phone in his hand, its cord stretched to its limits.

"It's Chris," he explains as he hands her the phone while she is pulling a maternity shirt over her head.

She has barely explained to the midwife what is happening when another contraction rips through her body. She drops the phone and grabs a towel bar for support. She watches, unseeing, and uncaring, as the phone skitters back toward the kitchen to release the tension on the cord. Michael picks up the phone and is describing to Chris what is happening while he walks the phone back to the bathroom door.

He picks up his watch and points at the dial. *How long?* he mouths.

She looks at the watch and tells him, "Two and a half minutes."

He relays the time to Chris and adds, "This was a long one." Waiting a moment, while Chris apparently talks to him, he then answers, "No, I didn't time how long the contraction was." He nods at the words Chris is saying and adds: "We'll see you in about 45 minutes." He goes to the kitchen to hang up the phone. When he comes back he is holding a large glass of orange juice.

"Drink this," he says. "It's gonna be a long day." He yawns and leaves her. She drinks all the orange juice, not because she wants it, but to appease him.

"I got the bag packed," he says when he returns to the hallway wearing his coat and carrying a duffel bag. "You better get your coat on. It's really cold outside."

As he is carefully locking the apartment door, he looks at her, and says, "Want to walk down the stairs? Remember, they told us in class that it would help to shorten the labor."

She doesn't answer him, just walks to the elevator and hits the call button. The thought of walking down four flights of stairs with the contractions that have been wracking her body scares her to death. She is imagining falling down the last few flights of stairs as another contraction doubles her over.

"You had to do this on the coldest day of the year," he says to her in the elevator. "Just remember, I'm the one who has to go out into the cold and get the car."

She waits in the vestibule while he goes to get the car; wave after wave of contractions wrack her body while she waits. She hears him honk the horn of her car and she walks into the freezing morning, wondering why she ever left Arizona. They drive toward the hospital, not speaking, the radio playing loudly enough to cover her grunts when a contraction hits.

He suddenly pulls over to the curb. *"I'll be right back. I didn't have time to make myself coffee, I was so busy taking care of you"* he says, slamming the door of the car, and heading into a deli that he frequents.

Not now, she screams silently. *I need you here with me. I'm scared*, she thinks as another contraction drives any sane thoughts out of her mind.

She counts eleven contractions before he returns to the car. She is doing the breathing exercises the nurse taught them in birthing classes, but she hasn't noticed any abatement of the pain.

"I told Jim what was happening and he needed to congratulate me," Michael says as he lets a draft of freezing air into the now warm car. *"He gave me a bagel and a coffee for the long haul ahead."* Michael holds up the bag and cup in his hand as he pulls the car back onto the street. *"Said it took twelve hours for his first to arrive and he got really hungry."*

When they arrive at the hospital, Michael parks the car in front of the doors and walks her into the lobby. The clerk at the front desk informs them that they need to go to the fourth floor and she motions to a man in white scrubs standing nearby. The orderly brings a wheelchair, she plops in it, and they head for the elevator. Michael goes back out into the cold to park the car. She is left alone with the orderly to take the elevator up to the birthing wing of the hospital.

By the time Michael comes back, she is lying flat on her back, a fetal monitor wound around her mound of a belly, a sheet covering her from the waist down, and a hospital gown on top.

"You're just in time." Chris says as he walks in, coffee in one hand and the bag with his congratulatory

bagel in the other. "I'm afraid I have some bad news. But it's not really bad." She pauses for a moment looking at the parents to be. "This baby either has a large dent in its head or it is coming into this world backwards." She smiles to show her lack of concern. "I'm pretty positive that what I feel is a butt trying to come out first. We need to do an ultrasound to confirm, but if I'm right, you need to have a c-section."

Michael falls into the chair in the room, barely managing to save his coffee. He starts asking a thousand, worried questions before the nurse comes in with a surgery release form. He grabs at the clipboard and pen the nurse is holding.

"She's having the surgery," the nurse says, pulling the clipboard out of his reach and handing it to her. "She has to sign."

"But it's my insurance that's paying," he whines.

By seven o'clock they give her shots to stop the labor and numb her from the neck down, then wheel her into surgery. She is so relaxed for the first time in weeks, that she actually closes her eyes, and rests as she is wheeled into surgery. A complete crew of aliens is assembled in the surgery suite. Garbed in gauzy gowns covering their clothes, poofy paper shower caps covering their hair, paper slippers over their feet, masks hiding their faces, and plastic gloves covering their hands. She sighs with relief when she hears Chris's voice and recognizes her eyes above the mask. Chris introduces her to the team assembled.

"I'll bring Michael in when he's ready," Chris says as she leaves the surgery suite.

Patient and delivery team are joking about surgery, comparing human and animal surgery when Chris returns with Michael. He is unrecognizable in his gauzy garb, but he comes to the table, takes her hand in his; his cup of coffee gripped in his other hand.

"I'm here for you baby," Michael whispers in her ear. "Don't you worry."

"Would you like a better view Michael?" asks Chris.

"I would," the patient calls over her belly that the surgeon is now cutting into. As they position a mirror for her to see, she looks at Michael and yells, "Someone grab him, he's about to pass out." Michael's face is the same green as the surgical gown he is wearing. Chris gets him a chair and he plops limply into it, dropping his head onto the surgery table next to hers, but facing away from the surgery. She is detachedly fascinated as the surgeon pulls a bloody, film covered blob out of the large incision he has made in her abdomen, with a loud slurp, and places the mass on her deflated belly. Chris cuts the film away and she can see the baby working to stretch out of the position it has been in for so long.

"It's a boy," Chris announces as she places Mikey on her chest. She longs to hold him to her face and smell and kiss him, but her arms will not obey. He has the look of a wizened old man that all newborns have, but to her he is the most beautiful thing in the world.

25

JOSHUA

Josh hears the opening bars of Mozart's Concerto #5 and fumbles on the window ledge for his cell phone. He squints at the bright sunlight that burns into the room when he disturbs the blind in the window. Sleepiness discards him when he sees his mom's private phone number on the caller ID screen.

"Hullo," he whispers, pushing himself up off the bed, and over the prone figure wound up in the bedclothes.

His eyes open wide and he stops, perched over the living mound in the bed, when he hears the voice on the other end of the line.

"What's wrong," he asks. In the years that Consuelo and Manuel have been employed by his mother neither has ever called him. And Consuelo is using his mom's private line which means she has taken the phone from Mom's office. Consuelo doesn't even clean Mom's office. The office is Mom's private space, not off-limits exactly, but HER space. He hears his heart beating in his ears competing with the quiet, accented voice of Consuelo.

"I was home yesterday," he responds. "But I didn't see her. I figured that she was in Phoenix with her agent or sumthin'. Was she home last night?"

Josh's eyebrows inch together and downward as he listens.

"I'll take a shower and head right up," he says, suddenly wide awake. "It'll take me about an hour and a half. Why doncha call Mike and Sean and see if they've heard from her. I'll stop at Cheryl's house on my way home and see if she's seen her." He listens to the the reply, then shuts down his phone with a frown on his face.

"What the fuck?" he says aloud, scrubbing his face with his hands.

"Wass wrong?" says a feminine voice from the . Mummy wrapped in bedclothes on the bed.

"Nuthin', Lins," he responds. "I gotta go home for a while. I'm gonna leave as soon as I shower."

He thinks she tells him to drive carefully, but he can't be sure, since he is already headed for the bathroom. His mind is pondering the mystery of his missing mom. Usually he loves to take Lindsay along to the small town where his mom lives just for the shock value. Her thirty earrings, nose piercings, lower lip ring, pierced tongue, dyed black hair, and the henna tattoos she recreates for herself weekly, always bring comments. But he doesn't ask her this time. He is focused on who else he should call to locate his mom. From what Consuelo said, she's been gone since yesterday morning, and hasn't left a message with anyone so far. This isn't normal.

As much as Mom would like to believe that she isn't, she really is pretty predictable, and has always let her boys know where she is.

26

MORGUE

"Signs of recent sexual activity," Ralph Emerson continues. Albright jerks his head around, sudden interest crossing his face. Ralph looks slowly over his mask at the now eager young face and raises one eyebrow. "I would guess it was consensual," Ralph's voice remains calm and even as he watches the interest fade in Roger's face, "since there are no signs of injury." Ralph's mind registers disgust at the young officer as he recognizes disinterest in Albright's demeanor again. *I hope you had a really good time*, he thinks as he looks into the blank eyes staring at him.

27

JACK

She can hear the faint bur-r-r of the phone ringing two thousand miles away. *I'll let it ring three times then I'll hang up,* she thinks. A quick glance at her bedside clock reveals the time to be 10:04.

"Shit," she says to the cat lying at her side. She starts to put the phone on its cradle, when a sleep deepened voice answers.

"Hey, baby," he drawls smacking the sleep out of his lips. "Doncha know what time it is?" But there is no anger in his voice.

"I'm sorry," she says quietly. "Go back to sleep. I'll call you tomorrow. I don't want to disturb you."

"Baby," his voice is clearer and picking up its normal speed. "You never disturb me except when you say 'good-bye.' An' I know that you have a good reason to be callin' me so late, so what's happenin'? You okay?"

She smiles and snuggles down into the pillows on her bed. "I'm okay. The kids are okay. I don't want to keep you up for no reason. I just wanted to talk."

"I'm lissenin'." he mutters. "'Sides," he speaks around a stretching yawn. "It's pouring out and I don't have to work tomorrow. Maybe not for a coupla days." He pauses to stretch and sit up in his bed. "What's up?" he asks, then a throaty chuckle travels the miles to her wanting ear. "Besides me, I mean."

"How long is it supposed to rain?" she asks. She can't keep the hope out of her voice.

"How long d'ya want it to rain?" his voice smiles across the wires. "Could be storming all week."

"Can you come out," she tries not to sound desperate. "The boys are on spring break. Sean is going to see his father and Josh is staying at school."

He is more than happy to get on a plane and fly out to the sunshine and warmth. It has been a cold, dreary, winter. They've only been able to see each other when she was in New York with her publisher, and the few times she's flown him out for short visits when the boys were with friends. The last time was only ten days ago, but it doesn't matter, they enjoy each other. He loves the sunshine and the carefree life he believes she lives.

She will pick him up the following evening at the airport, same flight, same time. They don't have to discuss the details. She assures him that the days are warm and sunny and the pool is ready for swimming in.

"Or other activities," she adds.

His chuckle is low and throaty. "Now," he says. "Let me get some sleep. I gotta get a flight early tomorrow and I have a feeling I'm gonna get a real work out when I get out there."

She places the phone back into its charger and curls down under the covers on her bed. One of the cats crawls up beside her and purrs. She is almost asleep when she suddenly bolts to a sitting position. The cat flies off the bed with a hiss and a glare over his shoulder. *This could be the last time*, she thinks as she falls back into the soft cushion of pillows. Tears roll down her face. "Do I tell him?" she asks. But there is no answer, only the cat jumping back on the bed, glaring at her, and staying beyond her feet to avoid being disturbed again.

Jack is a big man. Not fat, since he works and plays hard, but big enough to fill the seat of first class easily. He used to hate flying, but then he always had to fly economy, and those skinny seats just didn't suit him. He always felt like he was impinging on the person next to him, his knees would bump the back of the seat in front of him, and his legs would cramp from trying to fit his feet under the seat in front. He relaxes back into the comfort of the wide leather seat and sighs. First class and it doesn't cost him a dime.

"Another business meeting, huh Jack?" The flight attendant, Sylvia, smiles at him as she places his appetizer in front of him. The smile implies that she suspects he is traveling on something other than business.

"Yeah," he stretches out his jean covered legs. "Gotta take care a some things pretty often ya know?" They laugh together. Jack looks around at the usual "suits" in first class. They all have their laptops and cell phones out. They are all dressed in suits in varying shades of gray, most are under thirty-five, and look harried and worried. They are all drinking the free alcohol and many will have several more before the plane lands.

"Can I get you something else?" Sylvia asks. She already knows what the answer will be. It is the same every time he takes this flight.

Jack pulls his iPhone out of his carry on bag. It was a Christmas present from her. He downloaded all of his favorite music and loves the convenience of having it available any time he wants.

"Yeah, Sylvia," he says. "Can you wake me up about an hour before we get to the airport?" He puts one earphone in his ear then looks back at the blond woman smiling at him. "And bring me a cup of coffee, then, too?"

Sylvia nods and attends to her other passengers. Like every other flight, she serves him lunch, he sleeps, and she wakes him up an hour before landing to give him caffeine, so that by the time they land he is awake and alert. The last time he was on the flight, she told the other flight attendants she was going to follow him one day to find out who he comes to Phoenix to see. He is always flirtatious, but never inappropriate, polite, never drinks alcohol, eats the food without complaining. He always sleeps until they get over Denver, when he wants a cup of coffee or a Coke to wake him up. *She must be someone really special*, Sylvia thinks and turns to her less patient and more demanding passengers.

Jack doesn't walk to the carousel after he deplanes. He carries all he needs in his duffel, so he skirts the crowds milling around the silver snakes that will bring them their belongings, and heads for the north exit to catch his ride. Once outside he stops and turns his face up to the strong spring sunshine. It feels so good after the rain and clouds in New York. When he looks ahead again, he sees her walking toward him.

"There's my baby," he says and starts toward her. When he is about five feet away from her, he drops his duffel, opens his arms, and rushes her like a linebacker making a tackle. He picks her off the ground and spins around twice. When he sets her down, a frown creases his forehead, and he leans down to look directly into her eyes.

"You losing more weight?" he asks, running his fingers along her ribcage. "You know I like my women with some meat on 'em." With that he picks her up again and slowly kisses her shoulder, up her neck, and nibbles on her ear lobe.

She tries to squirm away, but he holds her tightly with her arms pinned at her side. Her complaints of "Do ya really think this is appropriate in public?" fall on deaf ears.

"Oooh," he whispers in her ear. "You taste soooo goooood." and as he puts her back on her feet she wobbles- weak kneed. She notices several people watching them now, most frowning with disapproval. She smiles and guesses they are thinking that she and Jack are too old to be acting like lusty teenagers in public.

"Wanna drive?" she asks holding a set of keys out to him. She usually drives from the airport just to let him acclimate, but his greeting has left her head spinning. Her conscience is still struggling with the need to tell him, and the reasons for not telling him. She still hasn't decided as she watches him return with his retrieved duffel.

"What're we drivin' today?" he asks. She takes him by the hand and points to the yellow Hummer dazzling in the sunlight.

"Wooo Hoo!" he whoops and raises a fist into the air. Then, still holding her hand, he runs to the huge vehicle, chanting "I get to drive a Hummer. I get to drive a Hummer." She is laughing at his enthusiasm. She once tried to pick him up in her hybrid car and he refused to ride in it. He claimed it would fall apart if he got in. He rented an SUV for the long drive to her house that day and since then she's picked him up in her truck. She hates the Hummer since it just screams "I can afford it!," is so big, and brings on so much attention when she or one of her boys drive it. But she knows that Jack will love its spaciousness and the stereo system.

She climbs in the passenger seat and he has already started the truck, is adjusting the radio station, the seat, and the mirrors, in that order. The moonroof is opened next. Then Jack adjusts himself into a comfortable position for driving using the many electronic buttons on the side of the seat.

It takes them over an hour to reach the gates of her ranch from the airport and they spend the time catching up on what's happened in the ten days since they saw each other. He tells her about the latest jobs he's working on and she tells him about her boys and the new book she's almost completed.

"Does this mean I hafta take time off to go ta Europe, again?" he asks with mock disgust. She smiles at him, but turns away and watches the city thin out to suburbs. Jack turns the music louder and talk is mostly suspended as they exit the highway.

"The thing I hate about all new vehicles," Jack says pounding the console separating them, "is they don't make bench seats anymore." He winks and smiles at her, "I want you sitting over here, next to me like we did when we were in high school." He reaches across the

110

expanse of the console to try to wrap his arm around her shoulders, "You remember bench seats? When you could snuggle with your baby while you drove down the road." She nods, shuddering; with the pleasure of the idea or maybe from the cold air blowing out of the vents of the vehicle's dashboard.

The gates to the ranch are closed and Jack opens the window of the truck as he pulls next to the silver box set directly at car window level. Instead of punching in the code to open the gates, he hits the intercom button.

"Hey," he calls loudly to the speaker, making faces into the screen above it. "Anyone home?" He gives her a sideways look and raises his eyebrows. "Looks like we've got the place to ourselves." He punches the code into the keypad and the wrought iron gates slide open. He slows the Hummer to a crawl and both of them revel in the view ahead. The long dirt drive that dips down to the low slung, adobe walled, red tile roofed house and the land that stretches to the foothills that border her property.

The house is cool and dark after the glaring afternoon sunlight. The dining room table is set for two with unlit candles gracing the center of the table. The smell of warming food permeates the air. Jack's stomach rumbles and they both laugh. She heads for the kitchen where their dinner is staying warm, waiting to be served, but he grabs her hand and pulls her to him.

"Food can wait," he mumbles into her exposed neck, holding the back of her head in both his hands. "I got something better for you than food." He puts her hand on his crotch where she can feel the bulge in his pants. His hands travel down her back and under the t-shirt she is wearing as their mouths lock together. He picks her up and unerringly heads into the bedroom and the soft bed that waits for them. He tosses her on the bed and lets her know without a doubt how much he missed her.

During dinner, Jack begins to yawn and she realizes that it is very late for him. They stack the dishes in the kitchen and she leads him back to the bedroom. Without pretense she drops the robe she wore at dinner and they fall into the bed again. This time the sex is sweet and slow and they curl into each others arms afterward. Jack is soon snoring softly and she is almost asleep when her eyes pop open. Wide awake, she carefully extracts herself from his hold, and dons her robe in the dark. On bare feet she pads out to the breakfast nook and carefully opens the door to the patio.

Outside she hunches her shoulders against the cool night air on her neck and puts her hands in the pockets of the robe. She feels something rectangular and stiff in the bottom of the pocket. She pulls out a pack of cigarettes and opens the top. There is one missing. At the bottom of the other pocket she finds the matches she got with the cigarettes yesterday. She pulls a cigarette out and lights it. The flare of the match momentarily blinds her, but she anticipates the feeling she knows is coming. The lightheaded euphoria just hits her when she hears the door behind her open. She turns to see a very sleepy Jack scrubbing his face with his hands.

"What are you doing, baby?" he mumbles between his hands. "Did I wake you with my snoring?" His look of concern is genuine. He steps out onto the cold tiles of the patio with his bare feet and winces, but puts his arms around her from behind and rocks her slowly. "I missed you. That bed is too big for just one person," he mumbles into the back of her neck.

"You're smoking," he says when the smoke of her cigarette rises in front of them. It isn't a question, but surprise, accusation, and concern rolled into two words.

"What's wrong?"

She so desperately wants to tell him about her visit to the doctor, but she can't bring herself to say the words. "It's Josh again." She lies and feels cold despite his body nearly wrapped around hers. He takes the cigarette from her and inhales it deeply.

"You know," he says finally, "the kid'll be fine. He's just going through a phase. He needs to figure himself out and understand that he's responsible for what happens in his life now. He's mad at you. He's not doin' anything that'll kill him or anyone else. He's just payin' ya back for what he thinks you did ta him."

And soon, she thinks, *he won't have Mom to blame for everything.* She shivers at the thought and Jack, thinking she is cold, opens his robe and wraps it around her. For the moment she feels safe and warm. They continue to discuss her middle son for the duration of their smoking. He has produced his own cigarette from the pocket of his robe and lit it after gagging on what he refers to as her "girlie cigarettes." She allows him to think that it is Josh who concerns her and vows not to tell him her secret until she has to.

"C'mon," he says after a pause in their discussion. "It's too cold to stand out here naked." He takes her hand and leads her inside.

But she still can't sleep, so when Jack has totally relaxed and is snoring softly, she rises, and redresses in the clothes she discarded on the floor before dinner. She goes to her office and her face is soon highlighted by the blue glow from her computer. Another task she realizes that she must complete soon. Her final book and she thinks it will be a good one.

They rise late the next morning and she makes a

big breakfast for him. She hopes he doesn't notice that she has no appetite. They spend the morning relaxing and in the afternoon she takes Sean's horse and Jack takes one of the quads and they explore the trails in the foothills north of her property. When they return to the ranch, she leaves him at he pool and she busies herself in the office until dinner time. She is surprised to hear voices when she exits the office and heads to the kitchen.

"Hola, *Senora*," Consuelo's soft voice touches her ears. "I thought you might need some dinner so I come to make it for you."

She looks at the two of them and their close proximity and realizes that this is not the first time they have met. She has always given Consuela and Manuel the days off when Jack comes to stay, but she should have known that the couple would check on her anyway. Consuela has been with her long enough to exercise discretion and the smile on Consuelo's face tells her that she likes Jack.

Dinner is an ecstasy of Mexican food and the two watch television before retiring to the bedroom for the night.

They spend a day exercising the Hummer in the desert trails. Jack revels in the vehicle's ability to cover the rough terrain. They picnic at a water hole, under some cottonwood trees and return home early in the afternoon. Jack wants to swim in the pool and soak up the sunshine.

"Do you mind if I have a drink?" she asks him.

"Honey," he answers. "I'll even make it for you."

She has a desire for Pina Coladas and while he is finding the ingredients to make them, she goes to change her clothes. When she returns she finds a drink waiting for her, replete with Maraschino cherry, pineapple, and a miniature umbrella.

"Nice outfit," he says soaking up her change of clothes with his eyes. "Reminds me of Jamaica." She is wearing a black bra top, a silk scarf at her neck, and matching silk sarong tied around her hips. The sarong extends below her knees, but the left side bears her leg to the knot tied low on her hip. She has a matching silk flower at her ear and a sly smile.

"That's where I got it," she says, sauntering over to the stereo to put on some music. "Remember this?" The speakers begin to throb with the beat of metal drums.

He is lying on a chaise lounge watching her. She drinks the Pina Colada quickly and pours herself another. Her hips begin to sway and her feet move to the beat of the music.

"Dance with me," she says, motioning with her pointer finger and swaying her shoulders.

"Oh, baby," he says with a groan. "I think I'll just watch from here." His eyes never leave her as she abandons herself to the music. Soon she is dancing back to him. She dances to the side of his chaise and pulls the scarf from around her neck slipping it behind his head. The dance continues with her gently pulling the scarf back and forth on his neck until he grabs both sides and pulls her closer to him. He caresses her left leg, reaching under the knot in the sarong. He realizes with a smile that the sarong is all she is wearing on the bottom. He reaches behind her head, and, with him still wearing the scarf, and her the sarong, they make love on the chaise. When they are sated, she rolls onto the chaise next to him and they are soon asleep in the warm afternoon sun. It is only when the sun dips below the horizon and the air turns cool that they wake up and move indoors.

They spend the rest of their time together on a drive up to Sedona and more sexual exercise. They eat wonderful food and both pretend that tomorrow will never arrive.

She walks in the bedroom to find him neatly folding the few clothes he brings and packing them into his carry-on bag. Tears spring to her eyes and he notices before she can turn away.

"Hey, baby," he wraps his arms around her and puts his chin on the top of her head. "Don't get upset, I'll be back again. You know that?" He kisses her cheek and turns to go back to his packing, but she grabs his hand and pulls him back to her. She reaches up to wrap her arms around his neck and gives him a long hard kiss. She can feel the bulge growing in the front of his pants as she pushes her body against his. His hands reach around her waist, under her shirt and begin to caress her skin. She slowly backs toward the bed, still rumpled from the morning's romp, and pulls him along with her.

Jack collapses face-down in the pillows and both of them lie panting, shaking, and exhausted. When he can trust his arms to move without violent shaking, he pushes himself onto his back, and reaches over to pull her next to him. She drops her head on his shoulder and they fall asleep.

Later that night, they take a bath in the whirlpool tub in her immense bathroom. He intends to relax and relieve tired muscles, but she has other ideas. When they finally fall into bed it is the dead of night and both sleep the zombie-like state of the totally exhausted.

Jack's plane is early the next day and he sleeps on the ride to the airport. His unshaven face, the bags

116

under his eyes, and his slow step are visible signs of the busy night he spent.

She pulls up to the curb to drop him off and he leans over to kiss her, cupping her chin in one hand. She presses her head into that hand.

"Hey, baby," he says in a ragged, quiet voice so unlike his own. "I'll call you when I get home." He exits the truck, turns to walk away, then spins around to face her again. He leans through the open window of the Hummer and with a wink says, "Anytime you want a night like last night," he slumps and hangs on to the window opening.

"Call me and I'll send someone younger, okay?"

She smiles, but her lips tremble and she turns her face away from him so that he can't see the tears forming in her eyes.

28

MORGUE

"On further vaginal exam I find two scars." Ralph lowers his eyes to look into the frozen open eyes of the woman on his table and speaks slowly and quietly. "Looks like she has at least three children, one born cesarean and two who caused her to have episiotomies...."

29

JUNE 3, 1987

"But he can't come yet," Michael whines. "He's not due for another six weeks."

"Never mind," she says. "I'll call Cheryl, and ask her to stay with Mikey, and I'll get a cab to the hospital, okay?"

She is more irritated than angry. She knows this baby is too early to be born, but she's been on the phone all day with the midwife, and this is apparently when he wants to come into the world. After she calls Cheryl, she calls her boss to let her know that she won't be finishing out her last two weeks of work, then she calls her mom and sister.

Joshua, she thinks while taking care of pressing business, *I'm going to meet you sooner than I thought.* She unconsciously rubs the mound of her belly. *I love you little boy*, she thinks, *please be okay.* The baby has been named since she was seventeen weeks pregnant, had amniocentesis, and she decided she wanted to know the sex of the fetus.

Cheryl arrives to stay with Mikey twenty minutes later with a whirlwind of questions. Cheryl has been her friend for many years, but never had any children of her own, and she is unabashedly curious about the birth process.

She packs the hospital bag and carries it to the car where Michael is waiting with the engine running. The midwife warned her that since Joshua is so early she can anticipate a lengthy hospital stay. Michael squeals the tires exiting the driveway and she clings to the panic handle above the passenger side door of her car. He is driving as if he is in a NASCAR race on the highway to the hospital.

"This baby isn't comin' fast," she says to him, gripping the panic handle with both hands. "You don't need to drive so fast."

"That's what you told me when Mikey was born," Michael answers. "And look how fast he came. And he was an emergency C-section, too"

"Yeah, I know," she says. "I was there. Remember?" She feels another mild cramp and takes a deep breath.

"Oh my God," Michael says. "Are you okay?" He drives even faster.

"Michael," she says, "I've had cramps like this for almost three months. This could be another false alarm." She tries to focus on the blurred landscape instead of the speedometer and her own fears about this baby's early arrival.

They make the twenty-five minute drive to the hospital in fifteen minutes. Michael parks the car and the two walk to the lobby from the parking garage, the overnight bag banging on her hip as she walks. The heat of the day is still undulating off the asphalt parking lot despite the fact that the sun has set.

As they enter the lobby of the hospital, Michael's pager starts to buzz. It is late enough that there is a security guard inside the door to the hospital. A waft of cold air envelops her and she stops walking to savor the feeling.

Michael suddenly reaches to her shoulder and pulls the bag off. The action is so unexpected that she nearly falls to the opposite side.

"Third floor," says the young security guard when they stop to check in. A real contraction grips her abdomen and she grabs onto the counter in front of the security station. The guard disappears around a corner and returns pushing a wheelchair in front of him. He nervously smiles at her as she plops herself in the chair. Michael drops the overnight bag onto her lap and they get into the elevator. Michael's pager echoes through the elevator.

"It's my sister," he says looking at the tiny screen that displays the caller's phone number. "I called her before we left the house. I'll call her back when we get you settled"

Rhonda, the midwife, examines her, and tells them that it is still a while before this baby will make his appearance, so they should walk to speed things up.

"Since the baby is so early, though, don't leave the hospital," the midwife tells her.

Michael stops at the nurse's station and asks for a phone to make some calls. The nurses direct him down the hallway to a pay phone. He takes her hand and leads her out to the pay phone, but when he starts to tell his sister what is happening she wanders away. Despite it being almost summer, the hall is cold and she wanders back to the maternity wing to walk. A contraction grips her as she approaches the window of the nursery. Michael finds her there leaning against the wall and doing her breathing exercises. As he gently rubs her back a nurse comes out of the nursery.

"It won't be long now." The nurse says as she watches them.

"Yeah," answers Michael. "We've been through this before. We know all about it." The nurse just smiles and walks down the hallway.

Michael's pager goes off three more times as they traverse the halls of the birthing wing. He has not convinced the nurses at the station to allow him to use their phones, despite his cajoling and whining, so each time he gets paged he deserts her. He has to call from the outer hall pay phone and converse with whoever is calling him from there, separated from his wife. The third time he leaves to make a call, Rhonda finds her leaning heavily against the wall in the hallway, swallowing the urge to vomit. Rhonda leads her into a labor and delivery room for an exam.

"You are eight centimeters dilated and he's engaged ready to come meet you," Rhonda says with a smile. "I think you'd better stay here and let us keep an eye on you."

Several hours later when labor has progressed to the pushing part, Michael's pager goes off again.

"It's my sister again," he says to no one and everyone. "I gotta call her." He leans over, brushes the sweat matted hair off his wife's forehead, and kisses her there. "I'll be right back. Don't go anywhere." He smiles at his own joke and leaves the room. She is secretly relieved that he is gone, he is no help to her, and she is afraid that she will punch him in the face with the next stupid joke he makes.

Rhonda whispers to the attending nurse. She can't hear what is said but the nurse nods, her eyes wide with surprise. The nurse comes back to the delivery room with another nurse and some wrapped instruments in her hand. "I'm going to have to do an episiotomy," Rhonda tells her between contractions. "This baby is so small and your contractions so forceful, I'm afraid that he might get hurt trying to be born. Don't push with this next contraction, okay?"

She just nods and tries to breathe the way they taught her in birthing classes, not allowing her abdomen to contract on the baby. She feels the needle sting and then a burning sensation as Michael walks back into the room. The next contraction grabs her with its power and she pants heavily concentrating on fighting the muscles that want to contract and push this baby out.

"What's goin' on?" Michael swoons in the doorway. The second nurse leads him to a wheeled stool and helps him to sit.

"I'm doing an episiotomy," Rhonda answers. "This baby is too small to push his way out without help."

She vaguely absorbs the conversation between Michael and one of the nurses. Apparently the maternity wing is abuzz with the idea of Rhonda doing an episiotomy. She has never done one before as she doesn't think it's a necessary procedure. She tries to make a mental note to discuss this fact with Rhonda when a contraction obliterates all thought from her mind.

Two hard pushes later, Joshua makes his squalling way into the world. The midwife hands him to her as Michael puts his arms out to grab the baby first. The midwife reaches past Michael and puts the tiny bundle into her arms.

"She did all the work," Rhonda smiles at Michael. "She gets to hold him first."

"You can only hold him for a second," the midwife warns her. "He's got to be put into an incubator and then fully examined by the neonatologist. But I thought you deserved to hold him after twelve hours of labor."

Joshua's big dark eyes stare solemnly into his mom's as if to give her a message. She falls instantly in love with the wrinkled, skinny, little creature and his pointed head, who is lying in her arms. She kisses his head to seal their pact. She checks out the slimy little bundle as a nurse puts a soft cotton hat on his tiny head. She checks to be sure that he has all his fingers and toes, and he reaches out to her with one tiny hand. Michael reaches in and sticks his finger into Josh's grip.

30

MIKE

"Damn," he says as he pushes open the airport door and his cell phone rings. The wind gusts at that moment and pushes him inside the terminal. He fumbles for his cell phone inside the heavy parka.

"Hi, Mom," he says after he checks the caller's number. His smile fades into a deep frown when he hears Consuelo's voice on the other end. In the years that she has worked for his mom Consuelo has never called him.

"What's wrong," his heart is choking him and he finds it hard to get the words out clearly. They talk for a few minutes while Michael takes his parka off, sweat forming under his arms, and on his upper lip. It is suddenly very hot in the terminal. Sean was right, Mom is AWOL and even Consuelo hasn't seen her. He looks at his watch and mentally figures out the time difference. It is still early morning in Arizona and Mom wasn't home last night.

"Can Manuel pick me up at the Phoenix airport?" he speaks quietly, but with authority. "Just have him use either my car or one of my mom's." He waits while Consuelo gets a pen and paper to write down the information about his flight and arrival time. There is silence on both ends of the line after Michael gives her the information, both deep in thought about what is happening. *"Hasta luego,"* Mike says then hangs up with a shiver.

He walks slowly to his departing gate and finds a seat alone in the corner. He couldn't describe the airport if anyone asked his mind is so focused on the situation at home. He takes out his cell phone and hits the speed dial to call Joshua.

I'll have to get Josh to do some checking before I get home, Mike thinks. *Then the two of us can work out a plan of action.*

"Hey, Josh," he says when his brother answers the phone. Michael is surprised that Josh is awake this early in the morning and sounds quite coherent. "Have you talked to Consuelo?" Mike is further surprised to hear that Consuelo called Josh even before she called him. Josh is already on the sleuthing trail and Mike has to admit to himself that he is impressed. He never expected it from Josh. They try to work out a plan to release Sean from their father's grip, but can't reach any good conclusions.

"I'll think about it on my flight home and come up with a plan," Mike finally concludes. Josh agrees since he intends to be busy calling everyone they know and looking for Mom. They decide to meet at Mom's house and spend the night; either to be with her or figure out what is happening. After all it could be nothing at all.

Mike ends the call and gets up to stretch. He paces in front of the uncomfortable airport chairs, anxiously dreading his boarding announcement.

"It could be nothing at all," he repeats to himself. But Mike's chest hurts as he listens to the flight announcements, he doesn't believe it is nothing. He feels something serious is going on or has happened. Mom has never gone anywhere without letting her sons know exactly where she is.

31

MORGUE

"One of the episiotomy scars is wider and less well defined, as if the cut and suture were done in a hurry..."

32

JUNE 10, 1991

She throws the magazine across the room and watches it hit the wall and slither to the floor. Two months of enforced bed rest is enough. Of course she hasn't actually stayed in bed the whole time. Who can stay in bed with four and seven year old boys running amok in the house? They'll be getting off the bus soon now, so she rolls to her side, sits up, and lets the blood rush out of her brain. When the dizziness passes, she stands up, and drags her bloated belly to the bathroom.

Late pregnancy causes her frequent trips to the bathroom, even more frequent with each successive pregnancy. This is her third, (last, she would tell anyone who would listen) and she wonders how the doctors think she can lie in bed and not make a million trips to the bathroom. One of the neighbor's daughters will be over soon to meet the boys at the bus stop. She had to hire her when she'd been put on bed rest. They'll have dinner together and Michael will pick them up when he finishes work. The divorce isn't final, but she is living in her own house. She only gets to see the boys when they get off the bus from school, for now.

That'll change after this baby is born, she thinks, and secretly hopes that this one will come early so she can have his brothers back with her. Until recently, she has never left either of them for more than two days, and that was for her mother's funeral.

When she finishes urinating, she wipes herself, and a glimpse of the toilet paper makes her want to vomit. It is soaked with bright red blood. She pulls herself up with the aid of the towel bar and looks in the toilet bowl. She inhales sharply at the sight. The water is blood red. Not tinged, but bright red. Her heart beating heavily, she reaches the phone near her bed, and calls her doctor. She calls David and asks him to meet her at the hospital. This is his baby after all. She calls Michael to let him know that she won't be home when he comes to pick up the boys. She meets Carolyn, the neighbor's seventeen year old daughter, at the door, relays the plan, gets snacks ready for the hungry boys coming home, and then drives herself to the hospital.

This baby is due in a month anyway, so now is as good a time as any, she thinks. She has to focus intently on her driving, like a teen learning to drive, as contractions have started, and she doesn't want to have an accident. Luckily, she finds a parking spot near the door to the maternity wing of the hospital. As she tries to rise from the seat of the car, a contraction knocks her back into the seat. She clings to the steering wheel, doing the huffing exercises that are supposed to ease the pain. When the contraction subsides, she grabs the window frame, and extracts herself from the car.

The walk to the birthing center door is about ten yards from her car, but it looks like ten miles to her. She waddles toward the building, feeling as if her pelvis is being stretched to each side, and she is clenching a bowling ball with her thighs. Though the lot is flat, she stumbles several times before she reaches the building. Once inside the building, she stops and leans against a wall. She is panting and sweating heavily as if she has performed a task of heavy labor. There is no one to meet her and the birthing center entrance is at the end of the hall. As soon as she catches her breath, a contraction knocks her into a squat. She balances herself with one hand on the wall and tries to do breathing exercises. When the wave of pain passes, she inches her way up the wall, and walks as quickly as she can to the birthing center desk. Sheila, one of the many nurses she got to know having spent so much time during this pregnancy in this wing, looks up at her.

"You're back," Sheila says.

"This time it's for real," the woman slumps against the reception area counter. Sheila rushes around the counter and swings a wheelchair at the laboring woman. The woman plops into it with a sigh of relief, enjoying the respite, until another contraction takes her breath away.

"I'm taking you right into a delivery room," says the nurse and pushes her toward the end of the bright and cheerful hallway. "Carol, we got another one coming," Sheila calls to another nurse in the hall. Carol races ahead to an open door. When Sheila arrives with her charge, Carol has the fetal monitor and bed ready. The nurses help her undress and get onto the bed. They circle the monitor belt around the woman's bulging abdomen. When Carol plugs the wire into the monitor the screen lights up and jagged green lines appear. Dr. Stocker appears suddenly and looks at the monitor. Another contraction convulses the woman.

"This is the real thing," Dr. Stocker says. "We're going have a baby today. Let's see how far along you

131

are."

"Four centimeters dilated," Dr. Stocker says as she peels off the gloves she is wearing. "I'll be back in about an hour. I have another mom here whose six centimeters dilated and you should go right after her." The doctor smiles at the woman in the bed and exits the birthing room, leaving Carol to attend to the laboring woman.

Her pains are a steady four minutes apart and Carol does another pelvic exam fifteen minutes after Dr. Stocker leaves the room. Carol's face registers surprise as she does the exam and the woman kicks at her arm to get the hand away. David walks in just in time to catch the nurse's look.

"Oh dear," Carol says with a bright smile. "You're eight centimeters dilated. I'm going to get Dr. Stocker." The nurse leaves her in the room with the labor pains and David. A fierce pain grabs her and she beats her fist on the bed side rail, clenching her teeth and suppressing a scream. She can feel the baby's head jammed in the birth canal.

When David tries to brush her hair from her face she punches him in the shoulder and swears epithets at him. She kicks at him as he walks past the end of the bed she is lying on and he moves to stand out of her reach. David paces around the room watching her from a safe distance, not knowing what to do. Beads of sweat form on his brow despite the coolness of the room.

Dr. Stocker and Carol arrive a moment later and Dr. Stocker does another pelvic exam. The doctor has to brace herself as the woman pushes with her feet on the doctor's shoulders to remove the offending pain of the doctor's hand.

"We've got a baby coming fast," she says not totally calmly. "Better get ready for it." She looks pointedly at Carol. The nurse leaves in a rush to return a few moments later with Sheila and a bassinet. Sheila is carrying some wrapped instruments.

"You're fully dilated and the baby is one hundred percent effaced." Dr. Stocker tells her patient. "With the next contraction I want you to push."

"Push," Dr. Stocker nearly shouts when the next contraction hits, "This baby is almost here." In an aside to the nurse she says, "Get me the scalpel, this baby is coming so fast he's going to tear her apart on his way out. I need to do an episiotomy." To her patient she says, "Don't push with the next contraction. Do your breathing exercises, okay?" The patient nods absently in response, her eyes focused on the ceiling tiles.

"Help her with her breathing," Dr. Stocker says to David, finally acknowledging his presence.

As the next contraction steamrolls the patient, David leans over to look directly into her eyes.

"Breathe," he says. They hadn't taken any birthing classes and this is his first child so David doesn't know what else to do. But she does. She grips his hand with an effort to break all the bones in it, and huffs quickly, concentrating on not allowing her abdomen to contract. A low moan emits from the woman's mouth, building into a shrieking crescendo. She just manages to avoid kicking Dr. Stocker in the head.

"You'd better get down here," Dr. Stocker calls to David, "if you want to watch this child come into the world." David rushes to the end of the bed, grateful for an excuse to release his hand from her deadly grip. He turns his head away when Dr. Stocker makes the incision, but returns his look in time to see the baby's head starting to show.

The woman starts to moan again, once again building into a loud "AHHH!" This time the woman clamps her teeth together, and focuses the energy of her yell into the muscles of her abdomen. She pushes hard, sitting up in the bed and Sean's head enters the world. The woman relaxes for a moment then sits up again to push. Sean slips, screaming, into the world. He yells while he is weighed, measured, and the neonatologist declares him a term baby with no inherent problems. Sean's screaming stops immediately when the nurse places him in his mom's arms. He burrows with innate knowledge until he finds the breast his mom is holding for him and nurses to sleep with a deep sigh. She is so enamored with this beautiful boy in her arms that she hardly notices the stitches she is getting.

33

JOSHUA

"Shit," Josh slams his fist against the dashboard of the car as he drives along the highway towards home. "Her cars were all there."

He pictures his exit yesterday evening through the garage and realizes what has been bothering him all night. All of his mom's cars were in the garage, Mike's WRX was in the carport and Manuel was using the truck. If she went somewhere she walked or went on horseback... But all the horses were in the corrals... Someone picked her up?

Something still nags at his mind, but he can't quite figure out what is bothering him so he turns the volume of the CD player up.

34

MORGUE

"She has a recent injury to her right ankle. Doesn't look like it was medically attended, though." Doctor Emerson says. "I can feel a chip from the ankle bone..."

35

A FEW DAYS EARLIER

She waits with her silent, broody son, Sean, at the gate to their property. The sun is shining brightly despite the shade over the bench at the gate, and both are hiding behind their sunglasses. They are waiting for Michael to pick up Sean for an extended visit.

"Do you have everything you need?" she asks the sullen teenager. She smiles at him knowing that soon he will grow out of this stage, be more comfortable with himself, and with her. He is her third and she is not worried about the sullenness.

"Yeah," he replies. He stands when he sees the dust from a car coming up their dirt road. "I'll see ya in a coupla days." He bends over to kiss her as she is still sitting on the bench in the shade of the ramada.

"I love you, Sean." She says as he walks to the car that has stopped and is waiting for him to get in. Sean turns toward her, taking off his sunglasses, so she can see his beautiful blue eyes. He runs back to her and wraps his arms around her in a rare hug.

"Love you, too, Mom." He has not said that in a long time and they smile at each other with the shared knowledge. He saunters to the waiting car and gets in the back seat. As the car raises dust in it's trek down her road she can see her son waving to her through the open window. She smiles and realizes he is growing up.

She punches a code into the keypad next to the gate and the gates swing open electronically. She enters the compound, mounts Sean's quad, and starts it. After a jerky start with too much throttle, the ride smooths out. A smile crosses her face when she realizes that it is actually fun to ride these damn things. Maybe one day she'll let her boys know that she really doesn't hate them as much as she claims. She races back to the hacienda to shower and get dressed. She has a doctor's appointment in an hour.

She parks the quad next to the other two in the carport and is headed for the house when she hears a squeal and bang from the horse corrals. Before she can get around the corner of the house to the fence, there is another loud squeal, a bang, and continuous rattling of horse fencing. She breaks into a run. Jamila is in heat, and is being a bitch to the other horses, but that wouldn't explain the rattling sound.

She opens the gate to the horse pens and sees Sioux nipping at Jamila's unmoving butt. Manuel is running for the pens, too. Jamila has apparently kicked at Sioux and jammed her delicate rear leg between the two lower bars of the pipe corral. Jamila is struggling to get her leg free and rattling the fence loudly.

Manuel reaches the stuck horse a little before she does and chases Sioux back into the barn closing the stall door. She reaches Jamila's head and starts talking to her quietly, rubbing the horse's neck and face.

Caballo loco, thinks Manuel. He would never say that to the senora since she seems to love the horse so much. The horse's leg is jammed between the horizontal fence rails, her hoof bent backwards over the bottom rail. The hock is swelling from the pressure of Jamila pulling to free her leg from the two rails effectively trapping her. Jamila must have kicked at Sioux through the rails of the fence and when she brought her leg back between the bars the hoof bent backwards catching on the bottom rail and the hollow of her hock jammed against the middle rail.

When they get Jamila calmed down, the two people work together to try to bend the rails, and extract the leg. Their combined weight is not enough to spread the rails and get Jamila's leg free, so Manuel leaves her to get a car jack from the garage. The woman stands at her horse's head to keep her calm. Before Manuel can use the car jack, she has him get Jamila's halter from in the barn. She'll need it to control the horse and assess the damage if any.

Manuel places the jack on the bottom rail near the horse's leg and extends it to put pressure on the middle rail above. When the rails bow enough, Jamila jerks her leg free, and charges forward. The woman, holding the horse's head, is not fast enough to get completely out of the way, and the mare steps on the inside of her ankle. She holds the horse's halter with her right hand, as it is the only thing keeping her from falling on the ground, and strokes the beautifully molded head with her left hand, talking incessantly. She can feel the pressure of her right ankle swelling, but she has to be sure that the mare is okay before she tends herself.

She walks Jamila to the wash rack and hoses the horse's hock and her ankle with cold water. Between hosings she walks the horse around and watches her progress from holding the leg up, not putting any pressure on it, to no sign of any limp or injury. She leaves Manuel to keep an eye on the mare, with instructions to call the vet if needed, while she goes into the house to check her ankle. Consuelo meets her at the arcadia door with a cold, wet towel.

She always seems to know, the woman thinks with a smile, sitting with a thump in the nearest stool at the breakfast bar to let Consuelo tend to her ankle. Her ankle is swollen, red, and very painful, but she can walk, and needs to leave for her Dr. Sands appointment right now.

"Oh well," she tells the upset Consuelo, "he won't be the first to see me in my sweaty horsey clothes."

Consuelo lets her friend leave only after she promises to have the doctor look at the swollen ankle.

36

MORGUE

Randy Albright hurries out of the room at the call from his superior. It's quitting time and Ralph Emerson turns away from the body of the woman on his table.

"Hey, doc," calls one of the many assistants walking through the hall to the exit. "Time to go home."

Home, the medical examiner thinks, *not since Sara died*. With a jerk he turns back to the body on the table. A frown deepens the wrinkles of his forehead. Sara had smoked the same brand of cigarettes this woman had in the pocket of her jacket. He remembers the months of coughing and vomiting she had gone through; her skeletal look when the chemo took away all desire to eat. And the pain that she tried to hide from him, but couldn't quite accomplish. He takes out the x-ray equipment and sets the body up for a chest x-ray. It's only a hunch, but his hunches are usually accurate. The majority of the staff has left, and he will have to develop the x-rays himself, but he feels the need to know if he is right.

37

BAD NEWS

She covers her face with her hands and the tears flow unchecked between her fingers. She suspected when she set the appointment up what the news would probably be, but it still shakes her to her marrow. Cancer. She hadn't quit smoking soon enough. The years of cigarettes replacing meals had taken their toll. This cough will never go away until she dies.

She can see the growing faces of her three boys reprimanding her to quit smoking for so many years. Especially Josh with his big brown eyes pleading and his chubby little hands and arms hugging her, around the knees when he was little, the waist as he grew bigger, and most recently around her shoulders.

"PLEASE, don't smoke, Mommy," he'd say as she lit up yet another cigarette. When she continued to smoke, he would walk away in a huff and not speak to her for periods of time.

Dr. Sands continues to talk calmly to her about

options and treatments and expected life span, but all she can think about is three very special young men who she does not want to leave. Mike always yelled at her to stop smoking. He never tried the cajoling that Josh did, but his sentiments were just as sincere.

"Don't you want to be around for my kids?" Mike would ask her.

When she finally quit several years ago, none of them said a word. She suspected that they expected her to start smoking again. They never chastised her again for all the years that she had smoked. The subject was simply dropped.

They are old enough to go on with their lives without her, but she wants to see them married, wants to see her grandchildren, wants to, at least, see Sean graduate from high school. Sean, who had only put up with her smoking for a short time in his life, would walk away from her when she lit up a cigarette. His feelings felt not heard.

"Can I call someone for you?" asks Dr. Sands interrupting her memories.

She shakes her head. "I'll be okay," she mumbles through the tears, and taking a deep breath, she hiccups the last of the tears away. She sits up straight and looks the doctor in the eyes.

"I've got a lot of things to take care of, don't I?" she says more bravely than she feels.

Dr. Sands nods, his eyes that professional look of practiced empathy. Someone who has given this kind of news before. "Let me call someone to help you."

"No," she says more sharply than she means. She

squares her shoulders, wipes her eyes with the back of her hand, and stands up to leave. "I can handle this." She stumbles as she walks to the door and Dr. Sands catches her arm.

"I'm okay," she says and gently pushes his hand off of her arm. She walks carefully to the door, then turns and smiles at the handsome man next to her. "I did this to myself, you know. I'll take care of it myself."

The doorknob eludes her grip and Dr. Sands reaches around her to turn it for her. She smiles her thanks and walks out of his office, shoulders back, head held high. Only her red nose and eyes give away the level of anguish she is feeling. She finds herself in front of her car without even remembering walking out of the building. She lifts her face to the bright sunshine and revels in the warmth. She loves this time of year; it has always held so much promise. She gets into the car and turns the CD player as loud as her ears can stand. She drives fast trying to lose the demons chasing her. On impulse she swings into the convenience mart near home and buys a pack of cigarettes. When she gets back in the car she tosses the pack and book of matches on the passenger seat. The rest of the ride home she glances at that pack on the seat inviting her silently.

Off the paved road, onto her own dirt road, she finally slows to a reasonable speed. The remote for the front gate and garage doors is on the visor and she pushes both buttons, swings onto the long drive, and watches as the garage door lifts to welcome her. She is driving very slowly now, trying to memorize every aspect of this oasis she built for herself and her children. She loves the way the tower of the entryway rises to bare visibility above the hill that conceals the rest of the house. She can just see the adobe tile roofs of the two massive wings that house the bedrooms. Cheryl's little house sits to the east partially hidden by a screen of ironwood and palo verde trees. She passes Manuel and Consuelo's house near the gate.

I have to make provisions for them, she thinks. She remembers the time that she picked up the couple from the convenience store in town where they were waiting to find day work. She'd been given a hefty fine, as it is illegal for residents to hire the unregistered day workers, but she never regretted it.

When she reaches the rise, before the land dips down to the big house, she stops the car, and reaches across to the passenger seat. Opening the cellophane wrapper enclosing the pack, she walks to the front of the car, and sits on the hood. She puts the cellophane in her pocket and scratches a match across the lighter strip. A spasm of choking makes her smile as the sulfuric smoke scratches her throat and lungs. She's already forgotten that you don't inhale when you light the cigarette.

The sun is setting and she lies across the hood of the car to watch the panorama of pinks, purple, and gold streak the sky. The cigarette makes her light headed and slightly dizzy, and she takes notice of the feeling, enjoying it.

She lets the cigarette burn itself out at the filter, and just lies on the hood of the car, watching the sky turn darker shades of blue. She is remembering taking care of her father, who died two years ago of lung cancer. He had been a heavy smoker most of his adult life. When he went into the army they'd issued him condoms and a pack of cigarettes. He'd been addicted until ten years before he died.

Tears stream down her cheeks clogging her ears as she remembers the pain he'd been in. He hurt so badly that he had punched her once while she was feeding him, knocking out a tooth of hers.

"I can't let my kids go through that," she says to the emerging stars. She pushes herself up off the hood of the car, and dizziness washes over her like a waterfall. Leaning against the car, she lets it pass, and watches the surrounding mountains fade into the darkness for a minute more. She gets in the car and drives home. She has phone calls and arrangements to make. She decides not to tell anyone why she is making these arrangements just yet. They will all know soon enough.

38

SEAN

Sean is thrilled to see Mike's phone number show up on the caller I.D. of his cell phone and answers the phone quickly.

"Mike," he says. "Josh just called and said you were coming home today instead of Saturday. Is it true?" He doesn't mean to sound so anxious, but he really wants to see his brothers, and go home for at least a day or two.

"Have you heard from Mom?" His voice cracks at the end of the sentence. His face shoots with red and he coughs to cover his embarrassment. Dad is watching him intently, so he turns away and speaks quietly.

"Yeah," he says. "I can do that." He pauses and steals a glance at Michael. Mike wants him to worm his way out of any plans Michael has and get back to the hacienda to meet him and Josh tonight. "I will. See you later." He ends the call, but continues to stare at the phone. He looks out the window of the hotel room at the many visitors playing in the hotel pool before he turns to his dad and the young woman sitting with him. Dad is staring at him.

"Hey, Dad," he says, keeping control of his voice so that it won't crack. "Mike wants me to go to Mom's house and spend the night with him and Josh before we all get together tomorrow. Can you drop me off?" He knows that Michael loves to drive by his mom's house and is always trying to get inside the security gate to see what she has.

"Why isn't Mike coming here?" Michael starts to ask when his cell phone rings.

Michael checks the caller I.D. and answers his phone with a frown. "Hi Mike," he says. Sean has to smile. Mike knows the old man too well.

Sean listens to the one side of the conversation that he can hear, and realizes that Mike is cajoling his father into seeing things the boys' way. Dad is putting up every argument he can think of without actually telling Mike no, but Sean knows that Mike isn't easily swayed. He learned his father's methods of persuasion a long time ago and knows how to get around each argument without damaging Dad's ego.

Sean smiles when he hears Michael say; "Okay, I'll drop him off about eight and we'll all get together tomorrow. I love you, too." With a deep sigh, Dad ends the call.

"Me and Laurie are gonna go out to The Horny Toad tonight," his dad says. "So, I'm gonna drop you off at your mom's house. That way you can spend some time alone with your brothers, okay?"

Good ole Mike, Sean thinks smiling on the inside

so his dad won't see his glee.

"Great idea, Dad," he says to the man looking at him.

"Then we can all get together tomorrow." His dad smiles and turns to converse with the young woman sitting on the bed watching television.

39

BROTHERS

With his backpack slung over one shoulder and a small duffel bag in the other hand, Mike pushes open the terminal doors to the bright desert sunlight. Mike's heart soars when he sees his mom's hybrid car at the curb waiting for him. For a moment he thinks that everything is okay, but then Manuel steps out of the car and waves. Mike's heart sinks back into the pit of his stomach. Michael can't think of a single time that anyone besides his mom has picked him up from the airport in Phoenix.

Mike and Manuel converse quietly in Spanish during the long ride to the ranch. It seems that no one has seen his mom for two days now, and no one seems to know where she might be. Mike gets more and more uncomfortable the closer he gets to home. He starts to drive faster when he turns off Carefree Highway. He is anxious to find out whatever he can.

The view from the rise in the long driveway entrances him as it always does when he first sees it after a lengthy absence. Mom did a great job designing the entire set-up. The strategically set flood lights make the house look inviting and spectacular. Even a few of the cacti have lights on them to enhance the beauty. Josh opens the front door to greet him and Manuel takes the car to the garage. Mike and Josh hug long and hard when Mike walks to the house. It is not a recently familiar action to either of them, but neither seems compelled to let go of the other.

"Sean will be here in less than an hour," Mike says, looking at his watch, and mentally figuring the time change. Then he looks up at Josh, "Let's discuss what we know so far, okay?

The two young men step down to the living room and situate themselves in comfortable chairs. The house is as Sean described it, spotless except for the phone, an open notebook, and Mom's personal phone book on the leather couch in the living room. The notebook has Josh's familiar scribble on it and a pen laced into the spirals that hold the pages together. Josh picks up the notebook before he sits in the chair and Mike grabs the phone. Consuelo comes out of the kitchen and hugs Mike with tears in her eyes. Mike consoles her in softly spoken Spanish and pats on her back. Consuelo wipes her tears away, smiles at Mike, and returns to the kitchen, where Mike can smell the enticing odors of her cooking.

Josh spent the day on the phone with friends and acquaintances listed in their mother's phone book. No one has seen or heard from her for at least two days. Mike is impressed with the thoroughness with which Josh has approached the task. Besides her friends, Josh called Mom's sisters, her agent, publisher, school, favorite students, the vet, travel agent, the farrier, and even the caretakers of the house in Vermont. No one knew of any plans she may have had or where she might be. Only her lawyer told Josh that she'd received a call from Mom three nights ago and they had discussed some serious

151

business that she wouldn't talk about over the phone. She couldn't come out tomorrow, but would be at the ranch in two days to discuss it then.

Mike asks Josh about a few more names only to find that his brother thought of them and called already.

"I just can't get into her computer," Josh says. "I tried, but she has everything password protected and I couldn't guess what the passwords might be."

Mike sighs and thinks, *At last something I can do.* Mom had given him her passwords at Christmas break so he could access the computer files in case of an emergency. He tells Josh about it.

"Well," Josh replies sarcastically. "I think we can consider this an emergency right?" His brown eyes flashing with anger.

They go into Mom's office and Mike turns on the computer. Josh sits on the antique trunk against the far wall staring at the ceiling or rug. He won't look at Mike or what Mike is doing.

"Holy shit," Mike says sitting up straighter in the wooden chair. "She's got a whole file on her and Dad's divorce. Copies of court papers and everything."

Josh can't pretend disinterest any longer and gets up to look over Mike's shoulder and read the computer screen. "Look to see if he hired a hit man recently."

Mike glares at his brother over his shoulder. So Josh hasn't changed after all. The two peruse a few of the more recent entries, but there is nothing to explain their mother's disappearance and Mike moves on to open other files. They even open the file containing first drafts of her books, starts of new books, and ideas for other books. Nothing gives them a clue to her whereabouts.

"I think when Sean gets here," Mike says leaning back on the chair with a sigh, "we better decide what to do."

"You mean like call the cops?" Josh asks sitting down on the trunk again.

"Yeah," replies Mike.

"I already did."

Mike looks at his younger brother with astonishment. He is about to comment when the front gate buzzer stops him. Josh and Mike walk together to the monitor for the security gate. Josh stands back to allow Mike to turn the monitor on. They see Sean on the screen and Mike is about the hit the button to open the gate when Sean interrupts him.

"Dad's here," he says. "He wants to see you guys before he goes out tonight." Sean moves away from the screen and their father's face fills the screen. He is wearing a big grin and trying to relive the seventies with his haircut.

"Hey guys," Michael says. "I wanna see you. Why don't I just drive Sean up to the house and we can visit for a while before my dinner reservations." He nods in agreement with himself.

Josh reaches over and turns off the gate screen. It is a security device Mom invested in to keep tiresome people away from her sanctuary. Their father can't see them and Josh has seen enough of his father for the moment.

"Well," Mike ponders. "We certainly can't let him

and Laurie onto Mom's property without her permission..."

"Let's get the quads and greet them at the gate." Josh says, a sly grin on his face.

Mike thinks a moment, then smiles and nods at the suggestion. He follows Josh out of the house to the carport, where the quads are parked. Mike isn't used to Josh taking such an authoritative stance, but he is secretly proud of him for it.

"You don' let that man in here," calls Consuelo from the kitchen as the young men head out the door. "*Senora,* she have court papers to keep him off our land." Both men nod and wave.

They each get on a quad and head for the entry gate. They are careful to stay to the dirt road carved into the pristine desert. There are low set lights along the drive that Consuelo must have turned on to keep them on the road. Mom likes her desert as natural as possible, no quads off the trails.

Mike pushes the remote opener for the gate as they approach and they can see Sean and their dad standing in the opening waiting for them. As if they practiced the move, the young men spin the recreational vehicles they are riding. Josh to the left and Mike to the right, effectively blocking the entrance.

Sean bounces in his sneakers until the dust settles from his brother's maneuver, then he runs to them. Mike hugs and holds on to the teen for a full minute before allowing Josh to give a cursory hug to his baby brother. All three turn to face the man and young woman at the gate.

"Hey, Dad." says Mike. As he hugs his father.

Mike can feel the much shorter man stretching to look over his shoulder. After hugging Josh, which Josh returns laconically, Michael stands looking past them at the impressive views of their mom's land.

"So," Michael says. "What's going on? How come you came home early, Mike?" He never looks directly at his sons, but stretches to look over Mike's shoulder to scan the vista beyond.

Mike turns around to take in the view his father is getting. Mike knows exactly what his father can see, as it entrances him every time he comes home, but he looks to let his father know that he has noticed the lack of attention to his sons. The long drive is vaguely lit by low lights and the tower of the entryway is all that can be seen of the house. Cheryl's house is well hidden as well; only Manuel and Consuelo's house near the gate is easily visible. As Mike watches, Manuel comes out of his house, a rifle cradled in his arm. Mike smiles and turns back to his father.

"Look, Dad," he says. "We just want to spend some time together. Just the three of us. Mom's not even home to bug us and it would be a good time for the three of us to connect. I'll take responsibility for the two younger ones and I'll call you tomorrow so we can set up some time for us to spend together. Okay?"

"Where is your mom anyway?" Michael asks without any concern or waiting for an answer. "Sure you don't want to go out to dinner with us?" Michael reaches over to the young woman standing near him and puts his arm around her shoulders. "We're going to the Horny Toad, and I know how much you all like that place..."

"We want to spend some time just the three of us," Josh visibly bristles. His brother's words about "taking responsibility" and "the younger ones" caused

155

him to sharply intake his breath and bite the inside of his lower lip. Now he just wants his father to go away and leave them to what they need to do. He'd take up the "responsibility" and "younger ones" issue with Mike later.

Sean walks over to stand between his two brothers and all three face Michael. Manuel steps behind the boys and into the light shining at the gate, the shotgun prominent in the crook of his arm. Michael steps backward, pulling the woman with him.

"But you said I'd get to see..." the woman starts to whine as Michael turns her away from the gate toward the rental car.

"I'll see you tomorrow," Michael calls out, a twitching smile crossing his face as he looks at the three young men, their protector behind them, and slowly retreats into the sanctuary of the car.

When the car vanishes over a rise in the road, the three brothers turn to one another, identical grins splitting their faces. They slap each other's raised hands in "high fives" then grab each other in a warm hug as Manuel disappears into the darkness.

"When did you learn to do that spin out?" asks Sean a grin splitting his face. "That was really cool. Perfect, like you practiced it or somethin'." Mike and Josh smile at each other and Sean's enthusiasm.

"Let's go back to the house and talk," says Josh. He keeps his arm around his younger brother. "You're riding with me." He nods to their oldest brother, "He can't drive very good. Lookit how he spun out here at the gate." All three laugh, mount the two machines and head back to the house. Their shouted discussions and laughter competing with the noise of the machines they ride.

Consuelo has made them a fiesta of their favorite foods and quietly leaves the house when they return. Mike grabs three beers from the refrigerator and hands one to each of his brothers. Sean looks shocked for a moment, but grabs the beer, and takes an unpracticed swig from the bottle. Josh and Mike share a wry grin at the grimace on Sean's face, but hide it from their little brother.

"Sumthin's wrong here," says Josh. His brothers don't even admonish him for stating the obvious.

"Sean," Josh continues. "When's the last time you saw Mom?"

Sean squirms under Josh's direct questioning. He can't remember Josh ever taking command of a situation and the two of them haven't spoken for almost four months. The last time he saw Josh was when he stormed out of the house at Christmas, screaming at their mom. Josh moved out the following week while Sean was in school. Sean knows that Josh has been back to the house on occasion, but never when Sean was home.

It is another moment of shock for Mike, too. Josh seems so mature and controlled. Not at all like the kid brother who tried to ruin everyone's Christmas revelry just a few months ago.

So the night long discussion begins. Sean saw their mother on Monday when she waited with him for Michael to pick him up at the gate. Josh last talked to her Friday at school before break began and Mike spoke to her on Sunday. She had not given any of them the impression that she had plans or appointments. The boys search the house, including their mother's computer files, again, but find no clues. The big kitchen calendar offers only the clues of a Dr. Sands appointment the day Sean left, and the letter J written in the next day's space.

All of her vehicles are in the garage or under the carport, the boys three quads are in their usual places and the horses are all accounted for. The house is remote enough that walking anywhere, besides Cheryl's or Manuel and Consuelo's houses, is not a consideration.

"Look," says Mike yawning. "I know it's only midnight here, but by my clock it's three a.m., and I am exhausted. I vote that we call the police and report her missing."

Josh grabs the phone lying nearby. He called the police earlier, but only asked if his mother had been involved in any accidents or incidents. The police had not been very helpful. This time the dispatcher agrees to send an officer out first thing in the morning.

40

MORGUE

Ralph's hands shake as he looks at the evidence on the x-ray. The viewing light creates a grey cast to his face as he stares at the obvious. It is all there, the typical interstitial patterns of lung cancer. One lobe of the left lung is completely solidified. He flicks off the light and returns to the body lying on his table.

That blow to the head did you a favor, he thinks as he gently touches the woman's forehead. *Lung cancer is an awful way to die.* His thoughts turn to his beloved wife, Sara. She died three years ago, but he is just now considering retiring since he has finally paid off her extensive medical bills.

"I'm glad you didn't have to go through it," he says aloud to the silent figure on the table as he puts the x-ray into an envelope. He puts the envelope on a corner of his desk without putting any identifying mark on it. He wasn't authorized to take the picture after all. Wearily he covers the body with a sheet and quietly says, "Goodnight, Jane Doe." before he leaves for home.

41

DAWN

"Damnit," shouts Josh as he walks into the kitchen and slams his fist on the granite counter. "Now I know what's been bothering me." He looks out the kitchen window into the horse corrals and sees Manuel's hat bobbing above the block fence. Sean crawls off the couch where he'd fallen asleep last night. Rubbing his face and squinting in the bright morning light, he looks quizzically at his brother.

"We thought Jamila got out by herself," Josh turns to his younger brother, a troubled look on his face, holding his arms out in front of him, inviting Sean to come to the same realizations. "She didn't get out on her own, Mom was out riding her." Josh pauses a moment to gather his thoughts. "The saddle is missing, not in the shop for repairs, but lost somewhere in the desert."

Mike enters the kitchen in time to hear this statement from Josh. He puts his hand on Sean's shoulder and the two watch their brother pace around the

160

kitchen, hitting his forehead with the palm of his hand, and muttering admonishments at himself for being so stupid.

"Doncha get it?" He looks questioningly at his brothers. "We thought Jamila got out by herself," His hands gesticulate and his eyes are wide.

"She musta gone out riding. Jamila came home without her and without her saddle. Mom's out there in the desert hurt or..." He stops suddenly and stares into his brothers' eyes. Only Mike's hand on his shoulder keeps Sean from backing away from the fierce look in Josh's eyes.

Neither Sean nor Mike is privy to the events that Josh is raving about, but Josh is spewing enough information that they get the drift. Manuel found Jamila out of her pen, the gate open, a saddle missing, and now Josh is adding it up to the conclusion that Mom had gone out riding the silly mare and was dumped by the horse.

"We should go talk to Manuel, then after the police come we'll take the quads and search the immediate area," Mike says quietly. The gate buzzer breaks into their common thought and Mike lets a sheriff's car onto the ranch.

Consuelo arrives just before the police car and she makes breakfast and coffee for everyone. Josh greets the officer at the door enduring the look of disdain at his long dyed-black hair, henna tatoos on his face, and numerous earrings. They settle at the dining room table and Sean drums his fingers on the tabletop. Josh stares at the officer as if waiting for a comment about his looks and Mike sits at the head of the table effectively taking control.

It seems that our mother is missing," says Mike.

161

"No one has seen or heard from her for three days now."

After taking a lengthy report from the three boys, including names, addresses and phone numbers of her friends and family, the sheriff asks for something to get a DNA sample from.

"Hair from a brush, a used toothbrush, nail clippings..." the sheriff looks at the boys.

"The brushes have recently been cleaned out, along with the rest of the house." His two brothers nod in agreement as Mike sweeps his arm to point out the spotless house..

"Hey, Josh," Sean looks at his brother. "Remember that stuffed dog Mom got for you when you were having trouble sleeping at Dad's house 'cause she wasn't there?"

Josh nods slowly, his eyes wide with amazement. That dog is at least twelve years old and Sean is only fifteen. How can he remember?

"Yeah," chimes in Mike. "It had a collar with a locket attached. Mom put a lock of her hair in the locket so that you would always have part of her near you."

Josh's face is crimson. He glares at his brothers then gives the sheriff an embarrassed smile. "I guess that hair would work for DNA, huh?"

The sheriff nods and Josh leaves to retrieve the toy. The stuffed toy is hidden under his pillow. He put it there when he woke up this morning and realized that he had been hugging the tattered toy all night.

When he returns with the stuffed animal, Josh tries to open the locket, but finds his hands are shaking too much, so he hands the toy to Mike. Mike opens the locket and carefully extracts the lock of hair from inside.

"Not all of it," says Josh watching his brother closely. The crimson color returns to his face and he looks down at the table in front of him.

"We only need a few hairs," agrees the sheriff.

Mike puts most of the hair back in the locket and closes it. He hands the stuffed dog back to Josh and places the hair in the envelope the officer is holding out to him. Josh unconsciously tucks the stuffed dog under his arm.

"Do you have any recent pictures?" the sheriff asks.

Sean jumps up from his chair and walks over to one of the bookcases in the living room. He pulls out a pristine book and takes off the dust jacket as he returns to the group now standing in the entryway.

"Her latest book," he informs them and shows them the professional picture recently taken of their mom gracing the back of the dust jacket.

"This is your mom?" the sheriff asks, looking suspiciously at the three young men in front of him. All three nod. The officer looks again at the dust jacket, the picture of the author, and the front cover.

"Is this some kind of publicity stunt?" the officer asks tilting his head to one side and giving hard eyes to the boys in front of him. There is stunned silence for a moment.

"My mom wouldn't stoop that low," growls Sean, throwing the unjacketed book to the tiled floor with the sound of a shot fired, and staring directly into the sheriff's eyes. "She doesn't need to, her books sell without any lousy tricks." Mike reaches over to place a hand on Sean's shoulder, but Sean shrugs him off, glaring at the officer and taking a step forward.

The sheriff looks up from the picture into three pairs of unfriendly eyes glaring at him. Sean is clenching and unclenching his fists, Josh is standing directly behind Sean as if to back him in a fight, and Mike steps between the officer and Sean barring any more advances.

"Our mom is an international best selling novelist," Mike says calmly staring directly into the officer's eyes. "She doesn't need to use cheap tricks to sell her books."

"Just asking," the sheriff says quietly and folds the dust jacket into his notebook. "We'll be in touch if we find anything." He starts for the door to make his escape,

"I need a number that I can reach you at," says the sheriff. "A cell phone…"

All three shout out their personal cell phone numbers as Mike's cell begins to buzz in his pocket.

"It's Dad," he says to his brothers as he puts the phone to his ear. He turns away from the others to speak in private.

Josh steps forward to provide the officer with all three of the brother's cell phone numbers, telling him to put Mike's number on the top since he usually answers his phone the quickest and they intend to be together anyway. Sean continues to glare at the officer.

Mike is still talking to his father when the officer

164

turns, again, to leave. Mike is obviously making plans for the three of them to meet Michael that evening. Sean and Josh listen closely as Mike discusses the evening's venue with their father.

"I forgot to ask," the sheriff turns and walks toward them again. "Does your mom have any distinguishing scars?"

42

THE SEARCH

The three young men watch the sheriff's car travel up the long drive until it's lost in the dust. They turn to look at one another and, without a word, all three head for the carport. Josh stops suddenly.

"D'ya think we should take the horses instead?" he asks his brothers. "It'll raise less dust and we can go as slow or as fast as want. They won't wreak havoc with the environment if we go off trail." His brothers give him wry smiles and he blushes realizing that he has just spoken his mother's words.

"I, personally, am too tired to handle a horse right now," Mike interjects.

"I think the quads will be okay," agrees Sean. "But if you want to ride Jamila, we'll keep ya in sight so she doesn't take off on you." Sean gives his brother a challenging smile. Mike tries to hide his smile, and watches and listens to see if Josh will rise to the bait.

A pall settles over the three of them when they remember their mission.

"Sorry," Sean mumbles. He starts to say more but Josh cuts in.

"No," Josh reassures his baby brother. "We got a job to do and fighting with a crazy horse is no way to handle it. Let's take the quads."

Mike's foot slips and the squeak his rubber sole makes on the floor causes the other two to look at him. He had been lounging against the stucco wall, feet crossed, arms crossed over his chest, a wry smile playing his lips, as he waited for the drama between his brothers to unfold. His foot slipped when he had to catch himself from falling over the shock of Josh's answer. Josh has never been able to back down from a challenge from Sean until now.

"So," Mike inserts into the quiet. "Let's roll." He feels the need to reassert himself as the leader. Josh is acting too mature and getting control of situations by shocking Mike and Sean too often. In the carport, Mike reaches into the old refrigerator to grab water bottles for each of them. He hands bottles to each of his brothers before heading for his machine.

The young men each mount a quad parked in the shade of the carport and start their machines. Sean is the first out into the sunshine, but Mike waves him back to the carport. When Sean drives the all terrain vehicle back on to the cement, Mike tosses him a helmet. Sean's face displays his disappointment in his brother, and he opens his mouth to say something when he realizes that both his brothers are putting their helmets on. He slams the helmet over his head, but leaves the chin strap unbuckled in protest.

With reckless abandon, Sean races to the back gate of the property. Mike and Josh follow at a more leisurely pace, both praying that they won't be taking Sean to the hospital today.

Halfway to the gate, Mike and Josh look at one another and nod. Both are being choked by the dust that Sean has raised and they simultaneously put on a burst of speed to catch their brother.

Outside the gate, Josh puts on a burst of speed then spins his quad to impede his brothers progress. He turns his quad off and removes his helmet. Mike and Sean stop when they reach him and follow suit.

"We forgot a plan of action." He looks pointedly at his brothers. Mike's shoulders slump in disgust at himself, but Sean looks quizzically at Josh.

"Do we have any idea where she might have gone riding?" Josh continues.

"She usually rides Overton Pass.." Mike says authoritatively, but his voice trails off. "Doesn't she?" He looks at Sean, and Josh, too, concedes to his baby brother's knowledge with a look of his own.

Sean fidgets under the gazes of his brothers, but realizes that neither of them has been around to really know where Mom might have gone. Sitting up straight and looking at his brothers in turn he says, "If Mom was riding Jamila..." he starts. Both of his big brothers nod so he continues, "She probably would have gone up Overton. She liked the work out the slope gave." Josh nods in agreement and puts his helmet back on. Sean does the same, but Mike sits and looks at his brothers for a moment before he dons his helmet.

All three restart their quads and Sean takes the

lead on the trail. Mike takes the left side of the trail behind Sean and Josh takes the right. Mike feels another jolt of surprise when he looks at Josh and finds him looking back. Mike can see Josh's eyes crinkled in a smile, before he nods his head toward Sean in front of them, then nods at Mike. Mike feels himself smiling back. All three enjoy the ride until the realization of their purpose sobers them.

They ride slowly up Overton Pass, looking for any sign of a person or saddle. At the top of the Pass they stop and pull off their helmets to gain a clearer view of the trail they just traversed.

"The only thing I saw," Josh says, "is the broken mesquite over there by the ironwood tree." Josh points down the trail where a flat rock juts into the trail narrowing it. He would have missed the broken mesquite, since it was on the left side of the trail, but the trail is so narrow that they had ridden single file, and he was looking down into the crevasse when he passed the ironwood tree. Besides, there is yellow tape pieces tied to some of the flora. Mike and Sean look to where their brother is pointing.

"Yeah," Mike says. "I saw it too. Couldn't miss it with the yellow tape on the cacti." He is not about to completely outdone by Josh. "But there wasn't any sign of a saddle or body..." He stops, realizing what he has just said.

There is a long pause as the brothers look down the trail. When they guiltily catch each others' eyes, they all turn toward the other side of the pass. Spread before them is a vast array of desert foothills crisscrossed with trails. They spot a mule deer foraging, and see quail and jackrabbits, but nothing else moving. They restart their machines and begin a long day of traversing trails. Each quad is equipped with a bag that holds energy bars, beef jerky and the water bottles Mike passed out before the ride, and the men stop only to snack on these.

As the sun slants deeply in the western sky, the three start back for home. They ride very slowly. None of them is willing to give up. It is a quiet, dusty trio that arrives back at the hacienda.

"I make snacks for you," Consuelo says quietly to them. "Go take showers and I will put them in de television room." Mike places a gentle hand on her shoulder as he passes her. Sean walks to his room with his right hand running along the wall as if to support his thin frame, his shoulders slumped, and head hanging. Josh stands in the hallway for a long time with a frown on his face. He can't bring himself to give up and do something as mundane as taking a shower.

43

SHERIFF'S DEPARTMENT

Sgt. John Reese enters the missing person report into the county's computer system and thinks about the three young men he met that morning. He doesn't truly believe that their mother is missing and he had driven his regular beat until twenty minutes before shift change. Those boys certainly don't believe that their mother is pulling a publicity stunt, but ten years patrolling an area dotted with celebrities and artists has jaded Reese's attitude. It takes him a full thirty seconds to realize that the computer is flashing a possible match to the information he just entered. He keys into the file and finds himself looking into a pale, tired looking version of the face on the book jacket. Reese pulls the photo he cropped from the dust jacket out of his notebook and holds it up to the picture on the computer screen. He doesn't really need to see the pictures side by side, he knows he's found a match, but he is delaying the inevitable reality. He knows where those boys' mother is: the morgue; listed as Jane Doe 48027.

Reese falls back against the chair and lets out a

long deep breath, he didn't even realize he was holding it until he exhales.

"Whassup, John?" Investigator Cruz puts a large hand on Reese's shoulder and looks at him closely. "You look like you've seen a ghost."

"I was so sure this missing person report was a publicity stunt…" John Reese mutters as he hands Cruz the dust jacket photo.

"Hey," the big man booms. "I know her. My wife reads all her books." He stops suddenly and looks at the photo on the computer screen. "Oh shit, you gotta be kiddin' me."

"And now I gotta call her three boys and have 'em identify and claim the body." Reese looks up at Cruz, pleading with his eyes.

"I don't envy ya," Cruz says. "Those are tough calls anytime. Ya always kinda hope that the old lady ran away with the pool boy or sumthin'. Good luck, pal." Cruz walks away without a backward glance, shoulders hunched and shaking his head. "Maria's gonna be so disappointed when I tell her."

John Reese picks up his notebook and flips to the page of phone numbers the pierced kid gave him. He grabs the phone and dials the first number on the list. While the phone rings, he thinks about what he will say to the boy who answers. He hopes that it will be the oldest one, since he seemed the least pissed off.

44

DUSK

Mike's cell phone vibrates just as the waitress sets his food in front of him. Sean, who is sitting directly to his right, jumps and looks at his big brother. Mike frowns at the caller's number.

"I gotta take this," he smiles at his father. "It's important." He looks pointedly at Josh sitting across the table.

Sean jumps out of his seat as Mike rises. "I gotta go to the bathroom," he croaks, following Mike out of the dining area of the restaurant.

"It's the cops, isn't it?" Sean looks up at his oldest brother, his face so pale that the smattering of freckles is standing in stark contrast to the rest of his skin.

"Yeah," Mike answers the phone as soon as they are outside the restaurant. Sean falls back against the posts and rail fence surrounding the outdoor dining area, his hands on his head, tugging gently at his hair. He listens intently to his brother's end of the conversation to ascertain the purpose of the call. But, he knows. He doesn't need Mike or anyone else to tell him.

"They think they found Mom's body." Mike looks ready to vomit and the fleeting moment of hope that Sean felt dissipates. "They want at least one of us to go down and identify her." As soon as the words are out of his mouth, Mike leans over and vomits on the desert landscape in front of the restaurant. Sean runs to his side and puts his arm around Mike's shoulders.

"It might not be her." He tries to soothe his big brother.

Mike stands up and swipes his mouth with the sleeve of his sweatshirt, it is his turn to be pale. "I think I should go by myself," he says looking at his little brother with telling eyes. "It's probably not her..."

"No way you're goin' alone," says Sean louder than he intended. "We're in this together." They stare at one another for a full minute.

"Let's go get Josh," says Mike, putting his arm around Sean's shoulders, and walking back into the restaurant.

Josh stands so suddenly, when he sees his brothers re-enter the restaurant, that his chair falls to the floor with a loud crash. The looks on his brothers' faces tell him all he needs to know.

"We gotta go," he says to his father.

"What is it?" Michael stands up and looks at the three boys. "Is it your mom? Is she okay?" He puts down his napkin and takes a step toward the boys, but is

174

stopped by the united wall they present. "What's..."

"We gotta go," says Josh staring into the mirror of what he'll look like in about thirty years. "This is our business." Josh reaches out, puts his arm around Sean's shoulders, they turn as one and the three brothers walk out of the restaurant.

"That was rude," says Laurie, as Michael plops back in his chair, and takes a long pull on his beer. "They didn't even touch their food." As if hearing this comment, Josh suddenly turns around, stalks back to the table, and pulls out his wallet. He extracts money from it, and throws the twenties his mother left for him on the table. He smiles at his father and Laurie then turns back to his brothers. Sean and Mike watch the entire transaction waiting for Josh in the entrance to the restaurant. They leave with their arms around each other, thankful that they came together in one car. Mike hands the keys to Josh when they reach the car in the lot. Josh doesn't ask why, he just unlocks the car and gets in the driver's seat.

The ride to downtown Phoenix is a quiet one; each boy lost in his own personal thoughts. Josh drives slowly and turns the radio off so that they can each think in peace. He parks the car in front of the Forensic Science Building as Mike directed him before they left Cave Creek. They sit in extended silence for a minute, before Mike fumbles for the door handle and gets out of the car. Sean pushes out of the back seat and they wait on the sidewalk for Josh to join them. Josh sits in the car, his head resting on his arms, his hands still on the steering wheel. Finally, he lifts his head, opens the door, and steps into the deserted street. He fumbles in his pocket and his hand emerges with a quarter in it. He starts to put the money in the meter when Mike puts a hand on his, stopping the motion. Mike points to the sign that says parking is free after six p.m. Josh looks at his brothers expecting them to laugh at him, but sees only understanding in their eyes.

"There's no door," Sean states the obvious. They are facing a multi-story red brick building with the words Forensic Science Building on the cement façade, but there is no way in. Josh turns and steps into the street as if to get back into the car.

"Wait," says Mike. "I remember now. Officer Reese said to walk to the south side of the building and enter there. The cop at the reception desk will page him and he'll escort us where we need to go." His brothers just stare at him, no one moves.

"C'mon," Sean takes Josh's arm and starts walking to the corner. Mike follows close behind. They begin the long walk into a world previously unknown to them and one that they wish they never had to experience. While the walk is long it is over entirely too quickly and they reach the doors. Mike opens the door and all three brothers hesitate, then enter the building side by side. Each young face echoing the look of his brother: fear, disbelief, and a spark of hope.

Their footsteps echo in the vast lobby, there is an officer behind the granite reception counter on the left and some glass display cases to the right. As if they had discussed it in advance, all three turn to the right. They stand together not looking at the displays of antique forensic tools.

"Can I help you," the officer calls to them.

Mike jerks upright and spins to face the officer. "We're here to meet John Reese." Suddenly, he can't remember the rank of the officer who was at the hacienda this morning. The officer behind the counter gives them a knowing look, a slight nod, and reaches for a phone.

Josh and Sean have turned around and all three stare at the revolving glass doors across the lobby. Josh finally breaks from his brothers and pretends to read the brass plaques on the wall. Sean and Mike continue to stare.

The three jump when the whoosh of the revolving doors announces the arrival of John Reese. The officer's face is grim as he beckons them through the door to a bank of elevators.

Josh's mouth is moving unceasingly, chewing his lower lip, and mouthing silent words as they wait for the elevator. When the four are ensconced in the elevator, the doors closing, his brothers can actually hear the words, "Please, God." Mike closes his eyes and slumps against the rail inside the elevator. Sean bounces, flexing and extending his fingers. He looks at every corner of the closed space as if looking for a way to escape. The elevator bounces to a stop all too quickly and the doors open. The three boys stare at the wall opposite the elevator, not moving, hoping that they can delay the inevitable forever. Officer Reese exits the elevator and waits patiently, watching them peripherally, instead of looking directly at them.

The elevator doors start to close and Josh reaches his hand to block them. He looks at his brothers, and Sean and Mike move to exit the elevator, Josh still holding the doors open as if ushering them out. Josh lets the doors go and steps back into the elevator. His brothers both have looks of pity on their faces. At the last second, before the door closes completely, he jumps out and joins them in the hall.

The floors downstairs are painted cement. The color is something between green and grey and very uninviting. The walls are tiled in high gloss puke green.

Easy to clean in case something splatters, thinks

Sean with a shudder that wracks his thin body. "It's cold down here," he says, rubbing his arms to cover the shudder.

Mike and Josh both walk to Sean and encircle him in their arms. It is Mike who breaks off first, looking at Reese to direct them. They walk down some halls, through some doors that Reese has to open with his pass key, and he stops them in a recessed area with curtained glass windows. The curtains are on the other side of the window and there is a small television mounted to the wall. The screen is currently blank.

"Wait here," John Reese says. "The picture will come up on the screen and I'll be back to get identification from you." His face is sad as he looks at the three young men assembled here.

45

REALITY

The medical examiner carefully arranges the woman's hair and pulls the sheet up to cover all but her neck and face. He closes the pale blue eyes and makes sure that the camera is pointing in a direction to avoid showing the deficit of the skull. He's been informed that three young men have come in to identify the body, the oldest being twenty-two. In his heart he knows that these boys are her sons and he is relieved that she will retrieve her identity, not be just Jane Doe #48027 anymore. He knew the first time he saw her that she was someone and had special some ones in her life. His conscience is arguing with itself whether or not to reveal what he found on the x-rays. He still hasn't written anything about the x-rays in his report. He suddenly decides to walk into the hall and see this woman's family for himself. He's rarely ever done this; his job is complete. He reported the cause of death and now she will be identified, but something compels him to see her family.

He turns the corner and spots the three boys standing in front of the screen that will give them a live feed from the morgue table. They are all good looking boys; not a surprise to the medical examiner. Two of the boys watch the screen expectantly while the third one is either looking at the floor or blankly staring at the walls. The tallest is apparently the oldest. He is tall and broad shouldered, short haired, and serious looking. *An Ivy leaguer*, the medical examiner thinks. The second boy, the one looking anywhere but at the screen, is quite a bit shorter than the first and, although they bear a strong resemblance to each other, the second boy is long-haired, and the medical examiner's power of observation allows him to see the multiple pocks left by piercings abandoned of their ornaments. *A musician or student* ponders Emerson. The third one, although taller than the second, is obviously much younger than the other two, pale skinned like his mother, but bearing a striking resemblance to his oldest brother. *Just started high school*, guesses the medical examiner, suppressing an urge to walk over and put his arms around the boy's skinny shoulders. They are a fine looking trio and he feels a stab of sadness grip his chest for them. He can already see the resemblance in all three to the woman lying on his table and he anticipates their reactions as the television comes to life in front of them. At first all that shows are dizzying lines tracing up the screen. Suddenly the screen snaps, and the face of what appears to be a sleeping woman fills the screen.

Mike stares at the screen looking at a pale version of his mom resting quietly. He waits for her to move or open her eyes. He finds he can't move, not even to take his eyes off the image he doesn't want to see.

Sean feels the tears coursing down his cheeks before he even realizes he is crying. He reaches out his hand toward the television screen, wanting to shake his mom awake. Even if she yells at him for disturbing her rest, he wants her to open her eyes and look at him.

"It's not her," yells Josh. "I knew it wasn't." He emits a harsh laugh and turns toward his brothers, a look of bewilderment crossing his face when he sees their faces. He walks over to his older brother.

"Look, Mike," he says, quietly now. "It's not her. Can't you see?" Laughing hysterically. "That's not my mom." His yell echoes in the room. The other two stare at him, and then step toward their hysterical brother.

"It's not her," he sobs, runs across the hall, arms raised. He runs directly into the wall, and collapses to the floor. He twists around as he slides down the slick tiles and sits on the floor with his arms crossed tightly over his chest. "Can't you see that?" His voice pleads with them to agree with him. He looks at his brothers as they reach his side and each puts an arm about him. "It can't be Mom," he croaks.

John Reese, waiting for positive identification from the boys, looks at the floor, and turns his back to give them some semblance of privacy. He's seen this reaction before, but still, it isn't easy to watch. His eyes register surprise as the medical examiner comes into the space where the officer waits and approaches the boys.

"I'm Doctor Ralph Emerson," he squats down on creaky knees to introduce himself to the boys. "Is this your mom?" He looks at the oldest boy squatting on the floor with his arms around his brothers. The young man nods and tears flood his cheeks. Ralph looks at the youngest boy and notes that he too is nodding his head, but refuses to lift his head up from the long-haired boy's shoulder. His tears have left a large spot on the shoulder of his brother's shirt, but neither seem to care. The one with long hair stares blankly at the floor, his eyes wide and dry.

"Is there someone I can call for you?" Dr.

Emerson asks the trio. The oldest and youngest boys just look at him for a moment, still holding their brother who is a quivering puddle on the floor.

"Just give us some time, okay?" the youngest one answers. "That's our mom." He nods toward the camera.

The officer signals for the camera to be turned off and leaves Dr. Emerson with the boys. He has a report to fill out. Despite walking on tiptoes, his footsteps echo hollowly in the tiled hall.

"How did she die?" the long-haired boy suddenly looks at Dr. Emerson squatting a few feet away. His voice is quiet and controlled, but his eyes glisten with unshed tears.

Ralph Emerson does something that he has never done in his long career as a medical examiner; he walks the three boys to a quiet sitting area, buys coffee and sodas for them, and tells them what he put in his report, about how he surmises their mother died. A blow to the head probably caused by a fall from some height. He talks to them for almost two hours, learning about the woman he has come to know more intimately than he wants, and his heart aches for the loss these boys are experiencing. He makes a conscious decision to never reveal what the x-rays told him. These boys don't need to know.

The boys stand as one to leave. They each shake Dr. Emerson's hand and thank him for his kindness. Dr. Emerson reminds them to sign the forms that Officer Reese will have for them around the corner to the left. Then they leave. They have a decision to make about where to send the body, but that can wait until tomorrow.

Dr. Emerson painfully pulls himself from the chair

he has sat in for too long.   As he tosses his coffee cup
into the trash can, he realizes that, for the first time, he
is looking forward to retiring and wants to go home.

46

LONG NIGHT

"We gotta lot to talk about," Mike says as he stops at the security gate in front of their mother's house. It is the first thing any of them has said the entire ride home. The car was so quiet each of them heard the other's cell phones vibrate. Mike shut his phone off, Josh just ignored his. Sean looked at the caller's number first, then threw the phone under one of the seats.

"And phone calls to make," adds Josh. Mike drove home since Josh was a mess when they left the morgue. Mike and Sean had to lead him out of the building and to the car. They put him in the passenger seat, buckled the seat belt and watched him all the way home. This is the first thing he has said since the morgue.

As they approach the front door, Sean bursts into tears. Both of his brothers reach out to him and enfold him in their arms, like the "group hugs" they used to do with their mom when they were younger.

"I'm an orphan," Sean wails.

Mike and Josh look at each other.

"Whaddaya mean?" asks Mike.

"I'm an orphan," Sean pushes them both away. "Both my parents are dead. Who am I gonna live with? Where am I gonna go?" He glares at his brothers. "You both still have your father. I don't have anyone." His face is red with the strain and tears pour unchecked down his cheeks.

"You have us," Josh says. "You'll always have us." He reaches for Sean and leads him into the house after Mike opens the door.

"I had a dream last night," says Sean still sniffling. Josh settles him on the couch and places one of the blankets folded over the back of the couch atop him. "I was searching for Mom everywhere. Finally I yelled for her and instead of an answer I heard a coyote howling outside."

"I had almost the same dream," says Josh dropping heavily into the nearest chair. "You know how Mom and I always played that game where I called her, she wouldn't answer, so I'd call louder and louder, finally yelling for her. When she finally answered I'd just say 'I love you' and Mom would tell me she loved me back?" He looks at his brothers and they nod with faint smiles on their faces.

"Well," Josh continues. "I dreamed that I was walking through the house calling Mom that way and when I yelled for her, instead of her answering me that coyote woke me up with its howling."

Mike turns away from his brothers. He has no

185

desire to add his own strange dream of last night to theirs. That damn coyote had scared the shit out of him when it woke him up.

"Phone calls or private talk between us?" he asks them.

"I think we should start with the phone calls," answers Josh. "I know that I'm not gonna sleep tonight, so we may as well get the calls outta the way and talk afterwards." His two brothers nod in agreement, and Mike goes to get phones from the three lines that Mom has at the house. Josh comes back to the living room with Mom's personal phone book. Sean comes back with three open beers in his hands.

"Good idea," says Mike spotting the beers.

The front door opens and all three boys look up in surprise. Sean hides the beer bottle next to the couch as Consuelo slips around the heavy door and stands in the entryway. The dogs seem unaware of her presence until she is at the steps leading to the living room. Though they are excited by her presence, even the dogs are subdued. Consuelo does not have to ask the boys what they found out, their faces tell her without a doubt. She sits abruptly on the steps, covers her face, and cries silently.

"You need food," Consuelo says, standing up after hearing about the boy's evening, and more tears are shared. "You have lots to do." She bustles into the kitchen and the boys can hear her getting out pots and pans, opening and closing the refrigerator, and running water. None of the boys think that they can possibly eat until she brings out a plate of her fabulous nachos and a bowl of fresh guacamole that she sets on the coffee table. Suddenly they all remember missing dinner.

"Senora give me some special phone numbers to call if anything ever happen to her." she says to the trio when they start to eat. "I will get them, and some burritos for you, then I leave you alone. Manuel coming to walk me back home, let him in, okay?" She leaves the room not waiting for an answer.

Josh is paging through the notebook that he started this morning listing all the people he called. The friends and relatives will need to be called first as they have some idea of what is going on. Mike is eating the nachos as fast as he can; his stomach empty after vomiting at dinner tonight. Sean gets up to answer a quiet knock at the front door and leads Manuel into the living room. Manuel stands humbly in the open area of the living room looking sadly at the gathering. Consuelo must have called him as he hugs each boy and waits for them to speak.

"She was out riding that crazy mare of hers," Josh says. He speaks so loudly that Consuelo comes out of the kitchen to listen, looking questioningly at her husband.

"That's why Jamila was out in the desert and such a mess the other day." Josh looks at Manuel. Manuel listens intently. "The saddle is missing because Mom couldn't tighten it herself and Jamila got out of it. I'll bet one of the bridles is missing, too." The three boys look to Manuel for confirmation.

"The one-ear bridle with the D-ring snaffle Mom always used." At this description, Manuel nods.

"Maybe the saddle slipped and she fell." Sean guesses. "Me or Manuel always had to tighten the girths for her before she could ride since her hands hurt so much lately." Manuel's face shows that he understands, and is starting to realize that what they are saying makes sense. It fits the actions of both his employer and her horse.

187

"Bet on it that Jamila spooked at something, the saddle slipped, and she lost her balance. Mom was too good a rider to just fall off from a loose saddle," Josh adds without malice.

The five gathered in the house look at each other and nod.

"But why wouldn't she wait 'til someone was here to help her with the saddle?" Mike looks perplexed. "She knows what a flake Jamila is and that she can't tighten a girth anymore..." He trails off.

Manuel looks guiltily at the gathered party, but no one seems to blame him. Consuelo, noting her husband's look of concern walks to him and takes his hand in hers.

"Believe that she die doing something she love to do," Consuelo smiles sadly. "All she ever want was to ride *los caballos* in her *montanas* and write stories." The four men in the room smile their assent.

Manuel mumbles, "*Loco caballo*," but all present hear and understand clearly. Consuelo is holding a small notebook, nervously turning it in her hands. She looks at it as if suddenly realizing it is there.

"These are numbers she left me to call in case something ever happen." Consuelo hands the book to Mike. "Your numbers are first, but there many other people to call and let know what happen." She crosses her arms over her chest and sniffles. "I think she list them in order. First to last."

Mike opens the notebook and notes that he, Josh, and Sean are listed on one line, then Aunt Gloria, Cheryl, an attorney, her agent, etc. The list goes on for several pages. All the entries are in his mom's handwriting listing a name and, directly across the page, a phone number or two.

It must have taken Mom quite a while to compile this list, thinks Mike. The names are neatly written and his Mom hasn't written this neatly since her hands became so painful. She uses her computer almost exclusively. He passes the book to Sean, who reads the entries then hands it to Josh.

"Time to let people know," says Josh and he picks up a phone with a sigh. "You want to just number each name one, two and three. Mike take the ones, I'll take the twos and Sean the threes." He looks at his brothers for confirmation. Sean doesn't even argue at being last this time. Consuelo retreats to the kitchen with Manuel and they can almost be heard conversing softly in Spanish.

It takes them until midnight to complete the calls on the list. Some messages had to be left and the boys agree to ask the people to call back for the news. Mike spent a long time on the phone with his father as his name and phone number were listed and numbered a one.

"Now, we need to talk," Mike says as he takes a long swallow from the latest beer that Consuelo brought him. All three of them have had a few beers at this point and Sean is looking sleepy until Mike says this.

"I know that Michael isn't my dad," Sean continues the conversation he started when they first arrived at the house. He looks directly at Mike who glares at Josh.

"I never told 'im," whines Josh.

"Duh, guys, I have a different last name," Sean says. "Besides, Mom told me about two years ago. She

189

told me my dad died when I was about three." A big tear rolls down his cheek. "I kinda remember my dad. I think."

"He was a nice guy," whispers Josh. "Mom really liked him and was really sad when he died."

Mike looks at his younger brother in surprise yet again. He can remember the constant arguments that Josh and David had the short time they knew him. He doesn't expect Josh to have this level of tact with Sean.

47

REVELATIONS

"We asked Mom if we could take you with us to visit our dad after yours died," Mike says to Sean.

"We never asked our dad," Josh fills in, smiling.

"We told Mom that our dad said it was okay for you to spend weekends with him and just brought you along."

"Mom dropped us off at Dad's house with you in tow one day." Josh says and Mike smiles at the memory.

"You were so cute that he couldn't say no."

"Besides we told him that if you left, we left, too."

"'Cause we're brothers," the older boys say in unison.

The three boys smile with genuine joy at the

memories.

"Mom was so pissed when she found out that we tricked her," says Josh. "But she talked to Dad and he told her that he was happy to have you. He wasn't really, at first, but he wouldn't let Mom know that."

"Yeah," Mike adds. "He acted like it was his idea all along."

"The best was the first time you called him 'Dad,'" Josh laughs a deep belly laugh that nearly doubles him over.

"I thought he'd have a stroke," says Mike. "He hated your dad. It musta killed him to have you call him 'Dad.'" All three boys laugh.

Sean can feel the warmth of his brothers' love, but is still perplexed. "Wha's gonna happen to me now?" He looks pointedly at his two brothers. "You're both old enough to live on your own, besides you still have a dad. What about me? I'm an orphan. Both my parents are dead." It is hard to tell if the beer or the emotions are slurring his words. "And I'm only fifteen."

Mike and Josh stare vacantly at the floor for a span of time, until suddenly Mike smiles, and looks at Sean.

"I'll adopt you," he says. Josh and Sean both look at their brother as if he has cauliflower growing out of his ears.

"Look," continues Mike. "I graduate in May. I can transfer to ASU, and get my Masters, and live here with you. Consuelo can stay here in the house with you until I move back."

"But, how can we afford to live here," Josh asks the sensible question. Mike considers being surprised, but he has had too many surprises tonight.

"On the trust your mom set up for you," Cheryl's voice startles them all into sobriety. None of them heard her come into the room. "Sorry to scare you. Consuelo called me and then let me in the carport door." She answers their unasked questions. She looks at the sad young faces staring at her as she balances a box on the back of the couch. "I'm also sorry that it is so late, but I figured you wouldn't sleep tonight. I got some things together, and then came over to be with you." She walks to Sean, who happens to be the closest, and wraps him in hug. "I am so sorry, baby," she says. The other two boys gather into a group hug with Cheryl and Sean and more tears are shed.

"Your mom left you all enough money to run this house for about ten years," she tells them when they separate. "If you're not extravagant." She looks pointedly at Josh who squirms from the attention.

"I called her attorney, and she'll be here tomorrow night." Cheryl picks up the paper sized box from the back of the sofa and drops it on the coffee table between the empty beer bottles and dirty dishes.

"This is her latest book, she just finished it. She left it with me the other night. I haven't read it yet, thought that maybe you guys should be the first." She looks at the brothers and adds quietly, "Since it's the last thing she wrote." Everyone looks at the box on the coffee table, but no one moves to touch it.

"She told me it's the best thing she's written." Cheryl's big blue eyes fill with tears. "She seemed so sad when she left it, but wouldn't stay and talk. Said she had too much to do." Cheryl pauses for a moment and swallows hard before she continues. "I guess that I'm the last one who saw her alive." She barely finishes the statement when the tears choke her. Mike puts his arms around her and lets her cry on his shoulder.

The jarring of the phone closest to Josh startles them all. Josh looks at the caller I.D. and answers it after telling them that it's Aunt Gloria.

"She'll be out tomorrow, too." Josh says when he hangs up.

"Gloria's the executor of the estate," Mike tells them. When his brothers both look at him curiously he adds, "Mom told me at winter break and we went through a lot of her legal stuff. I am twenty-two now, ya know?"

Consuelo and Manuel join the other four and they talk until the eastern sky begins to brighten. Manuel walks Cheryl home, and then returns to escort Consuelo to their little house. Mike has fallen asleep on the couch and Sean sprawls out on the floor with only a pillow to cushion him. Josh looks at all of them sadly and goes to his bathroom. When he emerges an hour later, his hair is back to its natural brown; he's washed off all of Lindsay's art work, and is wearing only two earrings.

"Mom always liked my hair long," Josh tells the sleepy Sean when he looks shocked at the new look, "Or I would have cut it, too." Sean smiles with understanding and drops his head back on the pillow.

Josh walks out the arcadia doors onto the patio. The moon still shines brightly enough to illuminate the land his mom loved so much. The mountains create a jagged edge to the lightening sky and the stars are winking out one by one.

"Mom," he says quietly. "Mom," a little louder.

"**MOM**," he shrieks. He turns around when he realizes that other voices have joined his. Sean and Mike walk over to stand beside him.

"Yip, yip, yow," the coyote answers.

"I love you, Mom," they call in unison and go back inside to get a few hours of sleep.

"Yip, Yip, Yowoooo," the coyote wails.

48

THE FUNERAL

The large house is packed with people milling about, holding drinks, and plates of the food. Mike walks among the crowd greeting each person, shaking hands, accepting hugs, and looking grieved. His suit is impeccable black, his shirt white with a starched collar, and his tie properly subdued blue with grey stripes. Sean sits in one of the leather recliners in a corner of the room. He is slouched and his suit, new yesterday, appears ill fitting and wrinkled. He's opted for a white polo shirt and no tie, as he knows that Mom wouldn't expect him to be too formal. He nods to the many people who stop to express their condolences, but has spoken to no one. Not even his cousin who sits next to him for twenty minutes trying to engage him in conversation. She finally gives up with a sigh, and goes to talk to someone more receptive. He refuses all food but will sip slyly from the bottle of beer hidden next to the chair. Mike secreted the beer to him earlier and he is grateful for that.

The front gate buzzes with another arrival and Sean uses the excuse to escape the pitying looks of his mother's friends and relatives.

"Hey, Sean," Lindsay's sweet voice comes over the speaker. "Can I come in?" She hesitates a moment, "I've got the band with me."

"Really?" Sean's voice cracks with surprise. "Of course." He blushes furiously and hits the button to open the gate. He is surprised Josh's band is showing up at a memorial service for his mom. They haven't practiced at Mom's house in months. Not since Josh moved onto campus and only came around when he needed money. Sean hasn't even met the new synthesizer player, but Josh told him the guy is phenomenal when they were together at Christmas. Until current events, that was the last time that Sean had seen his brother.

It takes Lindsay several minutes to travel the long drive to the house, and Sean waits on the front porch to greet her. It is a cloudy day, for a change, and he relishes the lack of sunshine. He doesn't recognize the girl who gets out of the driver's seat of Josh's car. She is short, slim, with pale clear skin, and beautiful long brown hair. It is only when she gets close, that Sean recognizes Lindsay's beautiful blue eyes, and can see the many empty holes from the multitudes of piercings in her skin. He's never seen her natural hair color or her exposed skin without a myriad of henna tattoos. Sean finds himself staring and appreciating what he sees.

Sean is further surprised that Lindsay is wearing a black tank top and a long black skirt. Her finger and toenails are painted a subtle pink instead of the usual black. Sean feels a stirring in his groin as she reaches up to put her arms around his neck and kisses him on the cheek.

Three young men get out of the vehicle, too. Sean recognizes the bass player, Collin, and Nick, the drummer.

197

He assumes the man with the long blonde hair, beard, and mustache is the new synthesizer player. Lindsay introduces him as Chris. The four are dressed appropriately for a funeral

"I'm so sorry," Lindsay whispers in his ear, giving him goose bumps all over. When she drops her arms and backs away Sean can see tears welling in her eyes. He wants to repeat the hug and steps forward to do so, but Collin steps between, and grabs him in a bear hug. Sean and Collin have known each other since he and Josh met in high school and they all practiced in the band room here at the hacienda.

"Where's Josh?" Lindsay looks sadly at Sean. She, too, has been a figure in this house for a couple of years. She and Mom always got along great, and she treated Sean like a pesky, but lovable little brother.

"Ain't seen 'im yet today," replies Sean. Lindsay looks worried, but walks into the house. She walks directly to Aunt Gloria and introduces herself. The two hug for a moment, talk, and then Lindsay seeks out Mike. They hug for a long time, So long that Sean, who is watching from a short distance away, feels the stirrings of jealousy.

Why doesn't she hug me that way, he thinks. He has had a mad crush on Lindsay since the band started practicing here. Lindsay sings and plays tambourine. She is also quite capable of using all of the sound and recording equipment in the band room.

Lindsay continues around the room, greeting each of the mourners. She has to tell most of them who she is since she looks so different today. Slowly she works her way to the hall where the bedrooms are located, walks directly to Josh's door, and enters the room. Sean can't see her any longer so he turns to Nick.

Lindsay and Josh appear from the hallway together. Josh is dressed in black jeans and a black polo shirt. His big brown eyes survey the room with all the people in it and he starts to turn around. Lindsay gently halts his retreat with a hand on his arm and he slumps against the nearest wall. He wants to disappear although he knows and likes everyone in the house. Knows everyone, it seems, except for one man.

Josh spies Mike and Sean talking in the corner of the living room and he joins them. "Who is that guy?" Josh points to a large man dressed in an impeccable black suit, white Armani shirt, with a colorful silk scarf hanging loosely around his neck. Mike and Sean look at the man, who is wiping tears from his eyes, and hugging Cheryl, Aunt Gloria, and Consuelo in turn.

"I don't think I know him," says Mike. "But Cheryl sure seems to." He looks at his brothers to see the same look of bewilderment on their faces. This is apparently someone who knew Mom quite well and they don't seem to know him.

"Wait a minute," pipes in Sean. "I know him." Both Mike and Josh look at him expectantly. "You guys know him too. He went on the European book tours with us."

Josh looks carefully at the man again. "You mean, Jack?" Josh replies squinting as if that will focus his memory more clearly. "Mom's body guard?"

Sean nods in response. Recognition dawns on Josh's face as the man turns to face them.

"Oh yeah," Josh finally replies. "I remember him. He wouldn't ride the horses in Ireland. Went from castle to castle in the supply wagon." The three brothers share a chuckle at the memory.

"He went to Jamaica with us last year, too." Sean adds.

"What is Mom's bodyguard doing at her funeral?" Mike asks no one, but he looks genuinely perplexed. The guy seems extremely distraught for a body guard and he seems to know Cheryl and Consuelo quite well. Mike rubs his face as if to erase the thoughts that are brewing in his skull. He begins to wonder how many of Mom's book tours this guy went on. He works his way over to where Cheryl and the bodyguard are talking in low voices.

"I can't believe it." The man sobs. "I was just here last week and she seemed so full of life," the bodyguard says softly to Cheryl as Mike approaches. The statement stops Mike in his tracks. He suddenly doesn't know what to think. This man wasn't a just a bodyguard, he was Mom's...

"Jack," Cheryl is introducing him to the body guard. "You remember Mike?"

Mike mechanically holds out his hand to the man. Jack's hand swallows Mike's in a gentle handshake.

"You were a lot shorter the last time we were together..." Jack is smiling at Mike, but tears are welling in his eyes. He suddenly grabs Mike in a bear hug that almost suffocates the younger man. Mike just stares blankly at the wall in front of him. When Jack releases him, Mike meanders to the kitchen counter and absently grabs a plate of food and a beer. He no longer acknowledges anyone else in the room, but the gathered people dismiss the attitude as grief.

Mike walks over and hands Josh the beer and plate of food. Josh gulps the entire beer and watches as Mike proceeds down the hallway towards the bedrooms.

He looks like a truck just hit 'im and he forgot to fall, thinks Josh watching his brother's stiff and jerky motions. Josh takes on the role of grieving son that Mike has vacated; greeting everyone, and accepting their condolences. He is talking to his favorite cousin when the eerie sound of organ music seeps into the occupied rooms of the house. As the music gets louder, conversation slowly ceases until all attention is focused on the haunting sound.

"Who invited Vincent Price?" asks Cheryl.

No one laughs, but several people nod. Chris, the newest member of Josh's band, walks down the hallway, slowly leaning his ear toward each door to find the source of the sound. When the next few strains pierce the gathering, Chris listens intently.

Nick and Collin watch Chris wander down the hall then they desert their positions at the food platters to follow. The music stops and restarts several times.

Sean runs out the open arcadia doors to the patio. He might have followed Nick and Collin, but several guests are now crowding the hallway, and he doesn't want to push his way through them. He knows the room Mom had built as a studio for them is virtually soundproof, unless the retracting walls to the patio are open. He surmises that the walls must be open for the sound to be so clear.

The glaring sun outside momentarily blinds him, but the patio cover offers shady contrast as he steps outside. He would be able to find the room even if he was blind as he has spent so many hours there practicing. He finds the retracting wall partially open and slips into the music room.

Josh follows Sean since the rest of the people are crowding the hallway outside the studio, leaving no room to even shove one's way through. Lindsay slips in behind them as organ music changes to piano and the synthesizer joins in on cue.

Mike nearly hidden sitting at the the bone colored grand piano that dominates the room. The container holding his mother's ashes is sitting on top of the piano. A book of music is slumped against the wall opposite him. Lindsay retrieves the book and notes that it is Elton John songs. Collin picks up the bass guitar and slings the strap over his head. Nick heads to the drums sitting next to Mike's piano.

After Lindsay puts the music book back in the bookcase, she turns on amplifiers and microphones. She looks sadly at the electric guitar sitting, gleaming on its stand. She presses the buttons to open the retracting walls all the way. Many people have made their way to the patio in curiosity and Lindsay thinks they deserve to see the show, too.

She turns back to the studio, and Josh is lifting the guitar that his mom had custom made for him. He touches the guitar all over, and stares at it with reverence, before he puts the strap over his head, and slings the guitar low. He stands staring blankly at the opposite wall, chewing on a guitar pick.

Sean walks over to the drums, and, without a word, Nick gets up from the stool, and hands him the drumsticks. Nick walks over to stand by Collin and Lindsay who are watching Chris.

After a few more false starts, Mike gets the notes he is begging from the synthesizer in the piano, and deftly switches to piano mode. Sean sits at the long unused drum set playing "air drums," and twirling the drumsticks. It has been a while since he's held the sticks and he needs to get the feel for them. Chris joins Mike with the synthesizer and Gloria puts her hand to her mouth and gasps. She recognizes the song and tears roll down her cheeks.

On cue, Sean joins with Mike and Chris. Josh is still slumped against the wall with his guitar hung around his neck, not touching the instrument.

Elton John's "Funeral for a Friend" fills the studio and wafts out onto the patio. The assembled guests watch in silence as Josh takes his pick from his mouth and joins in with his brothers playing. Mike stares at his piano, Sean at his drums, and Josh is still looking intently at nothing. When the song changes to "Love Lies Bleeding," Mike lifts his head to sing into the mic mounted on his piano.

"The ro....." he starts, but Josh's perfect tenor overpowers him and Mike stops, finally looking at his brother.

"The roses in the window box are growing way up high." Josh sings and looks at Mike. "Everything about this house was born to grow and thrive."

Mike and Josh smile at each other. Josh is singing the song his way. Sean and Mike join him in the choruses, as do many of the mourners. Josh grabs his mike, and walks it over to stand between his two brothers, his back to the rest of the people. Sean beats the drums with a ferocity that raises him off his stool, and the trio exchange looks ignoring the rest of the people. The final chords find the three sweating. As they finish the song, Josh falls to his knees, Sean loses one drumstick, then tosses the second one into the air, and Mike drops his head on the keyboard of the piano with a discordant clang.

Silence follows. Mike and Sean walk to Josh, still on his knees, and put their arms around him. While the rest of the mourners stand in stunned silence, the brothers hold each other and smile. Manuel, Cheryl and Consuelo slip out to the horse barn.

"Let's go set her free," says Josh. "It's time."

They look out the open wall and notice that sunset is painting the sky various shades of pink and purple. They stand as one. Mike grabs the container holding their mother's ashes, and they head across the patio to the barn

The saddled horses are waiting for them at the barn. Josh walks directly to Jamila and mounts before the little horse can dance away. Sean mounts his horse and Mike hands him the container holding the ashes. Several other guests mount horses and follow as Mike, Sean, and Josh head out the gate into the desert sunset.

Jamila balks as they approach the section of Overton trail that narrows. Josh has to pull hard on her mouth to keep her from running for home. Mike eases his horse next to Jamilla, effectively forcing the reluctant horse to face back up the trail. Mike then guides his horse past Jamila and Josh to take the lead. Sean allows his mount to nudge Jamila in the rear with its nose. With Jamila's nose in Mike's horse's tail, and Sean's horse urging her from behind, the trio is able to continue to the top of the pass.

Cheryl turns her horse sideways across the trail where it starts to narrow, effectively blocking the way for anyone who might follow the brothers.

They ride to the top of the trail, just as the sun

disappears behind the mountains to the west, and dismount. Sean pries the top off the container and Josh pulls something out of his pocket. It is three minuscule bottles with stoppers in them. Each bottle has a gold necklace attached to the stopper. Sean and Mike look at their brother with amazement.

"I want her to be with me always," Josh smiles a sad smile at them, pulls the stopper out of his bottle, and digs it into the ashes. Mike follows suit and does the same. When Sean tries to dip his bottle into the ashes he loses his grip on the container of ashes and nearly drops it. Some of the ashes fall to the trail and he stoops to scoop them up. Mike and Josh each gently grab an arm to pull him up.

"That's where she wants to be," smiles Mike, and Josh dips the bottle into the remaining ashes for Sean.

A breeze begins to blow and the brothers each put a hand in the container and toss ashes into the air. They watch as the breeze takes their mother's remains to the setting sun.

When the last of the ashes blows out of sight, the brothers hug each other. Crying freely they say quietly in unison, "Mom."

"Mom," louder this time.

"M-O-M," they yell.

"Yip," answers the coyote.

"I love you," the brothers call back.

"Yip, yip, yow," the coyote returns.

ABOUT THE AUTHOR

Eileen currently lives in New York with her boys and cats, hoping some day to return to her beloved Southwest.

Made in the USA
Middletown, DE
02 August 2017